Speak of the Devil

Shawna Romkey

www.crescentmoonpress.com

Speak of the Devil
Shawna Romkey

ISBN: 978-1-939173-19-5
E-ISBN: 978-1-939173-20-1

© Copyright Shawna Romkey 2013. All rights reserved

Editor: Melissa A. Robitille, Heather Long
Cover Art: Tara Reed
Layout/Typesetting: jimandzetta.com

Crescent Moon Press
1385 Highway 35
Box 269
Middletown, NJ 07748

Ebooks/Books are not transferable. They cannot be sold, shared or given away as it is an infringement on the copyright of this work.

All Rights Are Reserved. No part of this book may be used or reproduced in any manner whatsoever without written permission, except in the case of brief quotations embodied in critical articles and reviews.

This book is a work of fiction. The names, characters, places and incidents are products of the writer's imagination or have been used fictitiously and are not to be construed as real. Any resemblance to persons, living or dead, actual events, locale or organizations is entirely coincidental.

Crescent Moon Press electronic publication/print publication: February 2013 www.crescentmoonpress.com

Dedication

To my husband for believing in me when I didn't and my boys who are both angels and devils from time to time.

In memory of friends loved and lost
Mike, Tom, Steve
And Kelle

Acknowledgements

I am forever grateful to the following for helping me make this book a reality:

Romance Writers of Atlantic Canada, my writers group, for all of the advice and support. My editors, Melissa Robitille and Heather Long for their expertise and guidance. Steph Murray and Marlene Castricato at Crescent Moon Press for the big break and making my dream come true. My Beta readers Nancy Cassidy, Julia Phillips Smith, Sara Hubbard and Lori Jones. Tisha Hibdon Petree for being a cheerleader for years to keep me going. All of my past English teachers for showing me the way. My family for their patience and encouragement.

1 Dead

    I spent close to an hour getting ready for the party. I finally got to wear my new off the shoulder top. I belted it at my waist over a pleated black skirt and finished with my tall black boots. One look in the mirror and I almost changed back to jeans and a t-shirt. This outfit was a stretch for me. Usually I dressed more conservative, but Mike, Julie and I had been looking forward to this party for weeks.
    Not to mention the fact that Mike and I have flirted with each other forever. We almost hooked up at the last school dance, but I got super shy when he tried to kiss me. I pulled back the tiniest bit and that registered with him. He retreated. After our awkward night, we were back to "just friends" by Monday.
    This party promised to give us a second chance at romance. Julie, my BFF and Mike's cousin, was our biggest cheerleader. The three of us were always together.
    While parties weren't really my thing — I hated drinking, the taste, the smell, the drunken feeling — I could not wait for the party. I still felt like an outsider at this school anyway, except with Mike and Julie. I only moved here last year, so I still had that new student smell, and most people avoided me. I started here incredibly shy and withdrawn, but I had several of the same classes with Mike, Julie or both, and they were sorta quirky and weird like me. We were comic book, sci fi, and fantasy geeks, which was extremely unusual in the small country town we lived in, so we hit it off. Since

~ ☾ ~

my first month here, the three of us had been nearly inseparable.

I saw my reflection in the mirror and marveled at how much I'd changed in the last year. I never would have gone to this party on my own. If not for Julie, I'd stay home with mom watching re-runs every night. Julie never worried what other people thought. She did what she wanted and had fun every day.

While I hated some of the small-minded people we went to school with, this party was important. We were juniors and it was time we made ourselves known. We decided if we couldn't fit in tonight, then we would celebrate our misfit status and have fun being weird. It was important to me, and by association Julie, because I thought maybe Mike and I would finally cross the "just friends" line.

I checked the clock and wondered if I had time to change when Julie honked her horn out front. Panic attack!

It'll be fine.

It's not like wearing weird clothes could make the rest of the student body shun me any more than they already did or anything.

Besides, these clothes aren't weird. They are stylish, even if that pretty much means the same thing in this rinky dink town.

I grabbed my little black satin purse, shouted a quick "bye Mom!" and headed to the car.

A warm breeze hit me as I opened the door, so I tossed my jacket back into the house. School was almost out for the year, only 17 days left. *But who was counting?*

Julie sat at the helm of her ginormous Buick sedan and Mike stood on the passenger side and held on to the car door as though he needed to steady himself.

"Whoa," Mike said. I stifled a grin, as satisfaction

rushed through me. I'd made the right decision to keep this outfit on.

Julie struggled with her non-powered car window, cranking away to get it down. "You look great!"

"Thanks." I walked carefully down my front steps on my unusually-high-for-me black boots, while I gripped the handrail.

Mike jogged around the front of the car, holding out his hand to help me. He led me to the passenger seat he'd given up for me, closed the door and jumped in the back.

"Chivalry's not dead." I squirmed to get comfortable in the short skirt and high heels.

Julie awkwardly shifted the huge lever on the outdated Buick over the steering wheel into gear with a chunky clunk, and The Whale, as we lovingly referred to her car, lurched back out of my driveway.

"You really look great," Julie told me.

"Mmmm hmmm!" Mike agreed from the back seat.

She was a great BFF. We never competed with each other or felt jealous. It might have been a different story if Mike hadn't been related to her. Luckily it worked well for all of us.

"Thanks." I got a good look at Julie. She'd just worn jeans and a light blue t-shirt, which gave me a pang of fear again. "Maybe I overdressed a little." I smoothed my black skirt down.

"No way!" Mike piped up from the back.

"You look gorge!" Julie added. "I look like a bum, as usual."

I laughed at her. "You could never look like a bum." Blessed with long, thick, chocolate-colored hair and a naturally beautiful face, Julie rarely needed makeup. Her tall, thin frame promised a future as a model if she ever got out of our one cow town. She could wear a trash bag to the party and look great. But in Osage County that didn't matter.

~ ☾ ~

Her family didn't have a lot of money and didn't have the preacher over for supper. She didn't grow up here, so she was an outsider. Her parents were from around here but moved away before her birth. They moved back a year before I came. Her parents might be natives, but Julie wasn't. She started over at square one.

Rain fell, not uncommon for late spring in Missouri. "If you don't like the weather here," my grandfather would say, "wait five minutes." Of course, I'd visited distant relatives in Maine once before, and they said the same thing.

Julie fumbled with the wipers while I pulled the sun visor down to check my face in its little rectangular mirror, even though I'd only left my vanity like five minutes ago. The lights on either side lit up the interior of the car. I reached into my tiny party purse to find my lip gloss, which was easy to locate since I'd only packed the essentials in my bag: phone, some cash, and make-up. As I glanced at myself, I saw Mike in the reflection, smiling at me from the back seat. I stuck my tongue out at him, making him laugh, and put on the lip-gloss, fully aware of how flirty I acted.

The windshield wipers couldn't keep up with the sudden downpour. The pitter-patter turned to thumping. Hail came down in gumball-sized pellets. "Damn." Julie jerked the steering wheel to keep The Whale off the curb.

"Slow down, Jules." Mike gripped Julie's headrest. "We can pull over until it passes."

"Yeah." She squinted to see the road before her.

I pressed my lips together to smooth out the gloss. "Damn is right. I didn't bring a jacket."

The Whale swerved to the right crunching along the gravel on the side of the road. I braced myself in my seat. Julie leaned up to the steering wheel and peered over it as my grandmother sometimes did when she

~ ☾ ~

Speak of the Devil

drove. I squinted because of the stupid light up visor mirror. I slammed it shut, but Julie panicked and over corrected, pulling The Whale to the left and careening over the yellow dotted line in the middle of the street.

"Julie!" Mike shouted.

Time slowed and ticked out in heartbeats.

Ba bum.

Julie cringed, her hands moving up to shield her face. Her head turned away from the highway

Ba bum.

Mike reached protectively from the back seat.

Ba bum.

The headlights illuminated the rail of the overpass.

Ba bum.

The car hit the rail on the opposite side of the road with a hard thud.

Ba bum.

Crap. We're going over the bridge.

Ba bum.

The Whale's nose pointed down toward the water.

Ba bum.

A jolt forward and my forehead slammed into the dashboard.

Ba bum.

The Whale flipped in the air. *I'm upside down.*

Ba bum.

Pain.

Ba bum.

Did my mom say good-bye when I left?

Ba bum.

Cold water rushed into the car.

Ba bum.

Is this it?

Ba bum.

I can't breathe. Oh my God, I can't breathe. I can't see or breathe!

~ ☾ ~

My heart quickened. It pounded. The Whale leaned on its side under the surface of the water which rushed in fast, and I couldn't see a damn thing.

Calm, stay calm. Don't panic. They say when you're drowning not to panic because you use up your air faster.

Dammit, am I drowning?

I tried to get myself upright and jerked out of my seatbelt. Luckily, it gave way. I fought the latch to open the door facing up, but the pressure of the water from Black Water River held it closed, trapping me inside.

Jesus. I know this river. It's more of a creek. It can't be more than fifteen feet across and ten feet deep.

I pushed at the door. Opening my mouth to scream, I swallowed water.

I couldn't see or hear Julie or Mike. My watch ticked. Or was it my heart beating?

Ba bum. Ba bum. Ba bum.

Darkness.

Silence.

Cold.

Wet.

Defying gravity.

Nothing.

The dreams came. Like a good sleep you don't want to wake up from. I felt heavy and floaty. I wore this long white gauzy gown and the wind blew my dress and my hair like in some feminine hygiene commercial. I could breathe slowly and deeply. Completely relaxed and at peace, but I was alone.

I floated along in a white space for a while. Drifting. Breathing. Relaxing. Had I gone to a spa? After an immeasurable amount of time, others appeared. They wore white clothing, too, and they floated like me, reaching out. They opened their arms as if to welcome me to them.

~ ☾ ~

I stopped and frowned. I heard no sound, and I didn't know who these white floaty people were or why they welcomed me. They smiled, genuinely happy, and held their arms out to me. I panicked.

Where's my mom? My family? Wait, Mike and Julie were just with me, where are they? Are those wings?

I noticed the others floating with me had white feathery wings.

"Lily," one of them called out.

Holy hell. I'm dead.

***

I gasped for air and pain returned with the memory. Instantly cold and wet, I opened my eyes to a greyness interrupted by blurry spinning lights far away. I reached to see if I could clear my vision only to find a sheet covering my face. I pulled it down out of the way and tried to focus.

The spinning lights brightened, and rain spattered my face. I blinked and turned my head to the side. I felt heavy, like dead weight. I lay on the road on the hard gravel. My head pounded, and a loud ringing split my eardrums. I tried to look around to get my bearings, only to start coughing and choking.

"Jesus! She's awake, Sheriff!" Someone shouted. I tried to focus on the voice, but nothing made sense.

Several booted feet stomped towards me, spattering me with rain water from puddles pooled around me, and a half a dozen flashlights aimed in my face.

"God Almighty," someone's voice echoed nearby. "Lily? Lily? Look at me."

I tried but only saw a swarm of faces shadowed by hat brims.

"My head." I reached for it. Even my own touching it sent shockwaves of pain through me. Trying to speak brought on another wave of coughing.

"Turn her over!"

"Get the paramedic, now!"

They needed to quit shouting. It didn't help my head. They turned me on my side, and I coughed until an unusually long stream of water sputtered and poured from my mouth. Gross. Talk about embarrassing. *Have I been drinking?*

Someone patted my back. "That's it. Get it all out."

I obeyed. When I finally stopped coughing and caught my breath, I asked for them. "Julie. Where's Julie and Mike?" I didn't recognize my hoarse voice. My throat felt raw and shredded. It all flooded back to me.

Where I'd been. Who I'd been with. What happened.

No one responded. Maybe I hadn't asked it out loud, I wondered for a second, but then I focused on the men there. I didn't recognize any of them, but they were all dressed in uniforms of police officers and paramedics. The one who had turned me on my side and patted my back, wore a bigger hat than the others. The sheriff maybe?

"Julie and Mike?" I croaked.

He didn't answer. He just pursed his lips and glanced at the others. Sadness? Regret?

"No!" I cried.

"Honey, you're okay, but we want these nice folks to check you out." He spoke in a strong Missouri accent.

"No. Julie and Mike—" I pushed myself up to search for them and took in the entire scene. An ambulance, two police cars, and three more pickup trucks with decals on the side, all parked haphazardly with roof lights spinning madly, encircling the crash site. The twisted and bent rail on the side of the road pointed at the river waters below. And beyond, on its side submerged in the water with only its back two tires peeking above the surface was The Whale.

"Julie! Mike!" Those were the only words I knew. Hands took me by the shoulders.

~ ☾ ~

"You need to lie down until we can get you checked out."

I tried to free myself, but pain shot through my head and my shouting didn't help. I surrendered and looked the sheriff in the eye. "Where are they?"

He exhaled slowly, pursing his lips again, and gestured behind me on the opposite side of the bridge. There parked a white van. Just before one of the men closed its back doors I saw them. Two bodies on stretchers with grey sheets pulled up over their heads. Just like the one that had been covering mine.

"No, no! No!" I yelled and it felt like I tore my throat apart. I thrashed and tried to pull away from the uniformed men, but they held me. Fighting and screaming only made the pain worse, and the dizziness kept me down. Tears mixed in with the rain on my face, and they settled me back on the ground.

The van with my dead friends in it started up. My friends were gone, and I felt more alone than ever.

"I want my mom." My voice came out in raw, hoarse whisper.

A paramedic came to me. He checked my pulse and listened to my chest. He put an oxygen mask over my face which helped me breathe and loaded me into the back of the ambulance. The siren screamed to life.

They talked as though I wasn't there. I couldn't register what they said. Something about the car, my mom and eleven minutes. I kept hearing them talk about eleven minutes, but didn't know in relation to what. I shut down. They may as well have been speaking Japanese for all the good it did me.

The EMT climbed in the back of the ambulance with me, and the doors echoed the sounds of the coroner's van. I didn't know this person, but he looked down at me with soft eyes and a furrowed brow. He brushed a stray tear off my cheeks. I couldn't stop crying.

~ ☾ ~

"I know it's hard. Probably the hardest thing you've ever had to do. But right now, we just need you to live. You don't have to think about the rest. You just stay alive."

I am living, aren't I? Am I still at risk of dying? Or did I die again? He made it sound so easy. I had no idea how to stay alive. I closed my eyes and listened.

Ba bum.

My heart beat. I inhaled and exhaled and my heart *still* beat.

Good. Just breathe and be alive. I repeated the mantra as the ambulance sped, screaming me to the hospital.

The hospital stay was typical and more boring than I would have thought after everything I'd been through. My mom, family, and a few teachers from school visited, cried, prayed, thanked God. I lay there, not thankful at all. My mom brought our minister to see me on the second day. He went on about my good fortune and called me blessed. He even said I was lucky.

"Lucky?"

"Yes, to be alive. To have survived that horrible accident. According to the sheriff your heart stopped for several minutes. By all accounts you were dead, Lily."

"I don't feel lucky."

My mom patted my hand, probably hoping to quiet me. It didn't work.

"My friends died in that 'horrible accident.' Hell, I died. How is that lucky?"

"But you survived."

"And that's a good thing?" I laughed. It still hurt my throat to talk so much.

"God sent you back to us," My mom said. She took my hand and squeezed it too tightly, then patted and rubbed at it like soothing a fussy baby.

"My friends are dead and if God saved me, then He

~ ☾ ~

Speak of the Devil

killed them. I don't feel lucky." I pulled my hand back and turned away.

My mom murmured something to the minister and they shuffled out of my room. I tried not to cry again to spare my aching head, but I didn't feel lucky.

Not one little bit.

~ ☾ ~

2 Leaving

As I drove alone to their funeral, I thought of something silly Julie'd done. We tried on new clothes for school one day and used her back deck like models on the catwalk, taking turns showing off our outfits. Hopped up on caffeine and sugar, we were completely ridiculous. Mike popped in and watched, shaking his head the whole time. It was a total girl thing. His dropping by wasn't unusual, especially if he knew I'd be over.

We went in and out her sliding glass door. She came out in this hideous home-knitted disaster her aunt gave her for Christmas, trying to pass it off as a new school outfit, and Mike and I completely cracked up. She did the catwalk strut, sucking in her cheekbones, full goofy duck face mode. When she turned to go back into the house, she slammed right into the sliding glass door.

Mike and I stopped laughing and gasped, but Julie busted out laughing, and all three of us lost it. Whenever I thought of it, it made me laugh, just that embarrassed but amused look on her face.

At the funeral service I couldn't laugh anymore, which was for the best. When I saw Mike's mother standing at the side of his casket, leaning over, and fussing with his hair, I nearly lost my balance. I grabbed a nearby chair and turned away. I couldn't stand this much emotion. I couldn't bear it; the pain and the emptiness. I felt like a hollowed out Halloween jack-o-lantern, my insides scooped out. I stood there raw and empty, longing for my friends.

~ ☾ ~

"Are you okay?" I recognized the priest from St. Peter's. He put his hand on my shoulder to steady me and eased me into the chair. I felt like I should put my head between my knees to keep from losing consciousness.

I looked up at him. "Am I okay?"

"No, I know. Dumb question. We're all grieving," He sat down beside me.

"How does something like this happen? How am I supposed to go on? How does life go on?" The questions started spilling forth in an attack at the minister. "What are we supposed to do? I don't know what to do now." I started to shake.

"How does this happen? Where is God? Where is your God now? Does he even care?" I lost it and my voice started to carry. Father Doyle pulled me into his chest and hugged me, and then my tears came in waves.

I felt the blood rush to my face, as it always did to betray my embarrassment. This funeral wasn't about me, yet here I carried on as if I were the only one with a right to pain. As if Julie and Mike were my only reasons for living. As if I had a right to suffer more than their mothers did as they tried to fix their hair, so their bloated bodies would look better. They just weren't themselves without life coursing through them, and I barely recognized them.

Then the thought crept in that I tried to force back somewhere in the deep corners of my mind. That could've been me. That could be my mom fixing the hair on my dead, swollen corpse. I'd died and no one, not even me, knew for how long. I'd heard seven minutes and eleven minutes. I wasn't sure how they knew. I guess the police could tell by the clock in The Whale or the times that our cell phones stopped when they went under water compared to when they pulled me out and I coughed up half of the Black Water River. For a second I

~ ☾ ~

was glad. Glad not to be one of the ones in the coffin.

Thankful, but not lucky.

I was a jerk, a selfish, stupid jerk, I thought, and I just wanted to run away, but again, what right did I have to make a dramatic exit from their funeral with their family, grandparents, brothers and sisters, aunts, uncles there. I pulled back from the minister and fought the tears hoping I hadn't been causing a scene. I sat appropriately silent, though I screamed inside.

Once I'd gotten it together, Father Doyle smiled compassionately at me, and made his way to the pulpit. "The question that weighs on us at a time like this is: Why? Why them? Why two promising young individuals with their lives ahead of them? Why my son, or daughter, or sister, or brother, or friend? Why? Where is God?" He looked pointedly at me. "We can't answer. It is beyond our power to control and beyond our power to comprehend.

"But that does not mean we are powerless. How we respond when tragedy strikes is up to us. How we live after the heartache, that's within our power, and it's in these moments, through our actions, that we often see a glimpse of what makes life worth living in the first place," he went on.

"We must keep the faith. We must not define these young lives by their deaths. We must remember them as they were." He walked over and closed the caskets. "We must remember them full of life and love. Remember the love. Always the love."

I felt dead inside, and I knew first-hand what that felt like.

I left the service early, not knowing what comforting things I could say to Mike's and Julie's parents. Nothing I could say would help, so I just left. They probably didn't want to see me anyway. The one that survived.

I went back home to my empty house. Mom had to

~ ☾ ~

work, so I took some time to go through my things. I pulled out old photos of us, last year's yearbook, went through my laptop pics and e-mails, worshipped at their Facebook pages like they were celebrities, and searched for something... answers? Taking them in, their smiling, happy faces. Reading their words like they were inspirational quotes. Remembering and loving them.

In my search I came across the last post Julie had written on my wall, just some random thing she'd posted a few days ago. "You are beautiful." Tears stung the corners of my eyes.

Mike had written on my wall the day of the accident. We'd been emailing back and forth about some stupid math test I was sure I'd bombed.

"You're super smart. Don't sweat it. Besides, it's not the end of the world. Life goes on!" he'd posted.

"You always say that!" I'd written back to him.

"It's always true. You gotta have faith!" And that was it.

Typical. His and Julie's family was one of the churchy ones. But how do you keep something you don't even have in the first place? I'd died and some probably thought I'd gone to Heaven. I figured it was just some hallucination or dream from the blow to the head I'd suffered. Something programmed into our consciousness to dream of when we're out of it.

I turned to my dresser and looked at myself in the mirror. I'd put on makeup and curled my shoulder-length strawberry blonde hair. I would have looked nice except for the bruise and the gash on my forehead. I tried to cover it with my bangs, but it was there. A big reminder that I'd survived while they hadn't.

So many feelings overwhelmed me; sorrow, relief, guilt. I wanted so much to talk to someone about it, but Mom was at work, my Dad lived a few hours away, and the two people I would normally turn to were gone and

~ ☾ ~

wouldn't be back. For the last year, Julie and Mike had been there for me.

When I'd been nervous on the first day at my new school, they'd invited me to sit with them. They'd been the first to smile at me, the first ones to accept the stranger from out of town. They'd made me laugh. They'd made me feel comfortable and accepted and safe. They'd given me a place to just be who I was.

Now there would be no more Facebook posts from them. There'd be no more early morning chats by the locker. There'd be empty chairs next to me at lunch. They'd abandoned me, or I'd abandoned them. I'm not sure but either way the result was the same. Me, alone. Like it was before them. Mom and me moving. Her working and Dad across the state.

I didn't want to cry anymore, so I lay back on my bed. My head pounded again anyway. Soon I fell asleep with my laptop and photos spread around me. It wasn't even dinner time yet.

***

After the funeral things changed, yet they stayed the same. I couldn't stand either.

Everything was so quiet without them. The phone didn't ring constantly. The Whale didn't honk its outdated horn in my driveway. Julie's locker door didn't slam next to mine. Without Julie and Mike, I was an outsider again.

No one talked to me. Maybe they thought I would break down or get clingy. I drove to school alone. Went to my locker alone. Went to class alone. Sat alone at lunch. I did my best not to cry at school in front of anyone. *Our* classrooms, *our* lunch table, *our* steps we sat on outside when we got to school early. I went to all of them alone and remembered the white coroner's van doors closing on my friends forever.

Julie, Mike and I hadn't been big partiers which was

probably why we weren't in with the jingle jocks with their varsity medals ringing like bells on a sleigh horse as they walked or in with the pretty people, though Julie was definitely beautiful enough to have been. But even though we weren't at the popular lunch table, their deaths were felt by even the upper echelons of the chosen ones. When people die, sometimes those left behind romanticize the relationship they had with them. Suddenly everyone at school talked about how most of the football team had been in love with Julie and half the cheerleading squad had flirted with Mike daily. That couldn't be true. I still couldn't get a decent seat at lunch, so if Mike and Julie had been so desired, why did I still sit alone?

    I don't know. Maybe no one knew what to say or maybe they didn't want to upset me, but I was more alone than ever and not one person, teacher, student, neighbor, wanted to discuss it with me. Whatever the truth was, the pretty people acted like they were affected by the loss. Though they tried to make it about Mike and Julie and how wonderful they'd been, I knew they were just trying to get someone to feel sorry for them. Someone to console and comfort them. Some drama and angst to feel alive, maybe? Or maybe the accident scared them, made them realize we're all mortal.

    Whatever. I didn't care about them and how they coped and clearly they didn't care about me either. What I did care about was that they started drinking even more to ease the pain. Alcohol wasn't enough to smooth over the emptiness. Alcohol turned to drugs; marijuana, ecstasy, acid, I don't even know what else. Drugs were so far out of the realm of my reality it shocked me to be in the same room as they were. I had it in my head if I were ever to do drugs I'd be one of those people who thought they could fly and jumped off a building, or I'd end up chewing off my hand and have to go around the rest of my life with no hand, having to explain. Drugs scared me to death.

In math, Mike's desk sat empty now, and the ignorant ass teacher didn't even think maybe we could have a new seating arrangement, so this glaring, empty, screaming void could get shuffled around, and this silent desk would no longer be Mike's, but just a random extra at the back of the room. But she didn't. She left it, sitting empty beside me, so every day I had to remember him. The last time we'd sat next to each other in those chairs, he'd drawn a smiley face on the corner of my desk. Every time I sat down, I had to trace it with my finger. My eyes would sting with tears, so I contemplated erasing it, but I couldn't. I just couldn't. I tried to focus on class, but things like that, all of the tiny memories that seemed pretty insignificant at the time, kept creeping into my head.

I couldn't handle it. I couldn't think. I couldn't study. I couldn't socialize. Maybe I had died and stayed dead. Why had I come back? Why had I survived? Most times I wished I hadn't.

The school year ended, uneventfully for me, and summer began. My almost boyfriend and my very best friend were gone, and the people left around me changed into bigger drunks and drug heads than they had been before. I had to leave. A summer with no friends and everyone getting wasted around me was more than I could bear. The small town where everyone went to church and knew everyone else had been broken by this catastrophic event. In a school with a population of only a hundred to begin with, two fun-loving teenagers missing left a huge gap.

So rather than be the pooper at the summer parties I probably wouldn't get invited to anyway, I decided to leave. But did anyone notice? Did anyone care? Or were they too busy mourning for two people they wouldn't

~ ☾ ~

Speak of the Devil

have given the time of day to a few weeks ago?

I came up with the idea to leave my mom and my dog, which was terribly difficult, especially since I knew mom wouldn't understand it wasn't about her and would think I'd rather be with my dad. She didn't understand why I couldn't just get over it because she didn't have to sit by the screaming, empty chair in math, and I couldn't put it into words.

"The school in Kansas City has more opportunities, classes they don't offer here," I told her, so she wouldn't feel bad. I thought too, when I moved it would be great not to know anyone. I wouldn't have anyone I would have to dodge, or be self-conscious about not drinking, smoking or doing drugs with. I wouldn't be avoided because people didn't know how to talk to me. I could just stay home, study, and focus on me.

I needed to forget.

I needed to leave. I packed up my little Chevy with all of my clothes and a few boxes of things. I put on my pageboy hat I'd bought thinking how cool I would look; I was always too embarrassed to actually wear it where someone would see me. A two and half hour drive all alone was the perfect time to wear it, rather than pack it where it would get crushed. Then I'd arrive in KC cute and stylish and maybe just reinvent myself. I tried to make it an adventure.

I went inside to tell Mom I was packed and ready to go. She wanted to walk me out for hugs and good-byes. Not my favorite part, but it was a necessary evil. When I came back outside with her, Dusty, my collie, had jumped into the front seat of my car ready to go. He looked miserable. That was the last straw. My exciting adventure and hopes of looking to start a new life switched to doubt and fear and utter sadness. I lost it and turned into a sobbing mess. My mom broke down with me and if dogs cried, Dusty would've been sobbing, too.

~ ☾ ~

But it had to be done, crying messes or not. In minutes I was on the highway, headed for my dad's. Each mile I let go of something from my small town, some good things, some bad. I drove past the school we'd attended and where we'd gone to basketball games together. I drove past the church where we'd gone to dances and dinners together. I drove past the road that went to Julie's house where we'd always walk after school, the road that went to the accident site where we'd died. I let go of it all. A dog, a mom, a dead friend, a dead almost boyfriend, drinking, drugs, an empty desk, a smiley face.

And I kept driving, down the highway to my Dad's where I'd be living, to my new school where I'd finish my high school years, to all of the new places I'd discover and go on my own...

By the time I arrived in Kansas City, I had nothing but a clean slate to start with.

And a cute hat.

~ ☾ ~

3 Starting Over

Don't get me wrong, just upping and leaving my mom to move to my dad's wasn't an easy transition. I went from living in a small town to the city. From an old country farmhouse to a large suburban home in a ritzy neighborhood. From just Mom and me, to my Dad, step-mom, 13 year old stepbrother, 5 year old half-sister and me. All of us would need time to adjust to say the least. My Dad and step-mom hadn't had to really deal with a teenager yet. They were on the brink with Owen, but being on the edge and being smack dab in the middle of it were two different things.

I tried to leave my problems back in the country, but some of them just seemed to hang around me. They stuck to my aura, wherever I went. I came with physical and emotional baggage. I had sadness enough to go around. I ran away from it, tried to leave it in mid-Missouri, but no such luck.

Again, the new parental units were probably not prepared for the emotion and didn't entirely understand the healing I needed to go through. Neither did I, to be honest. I just knew how I felt sucked, and I didn't want to feel the void forever.

I arrived and settled in. Living in a family situation would definitely take some getting used to. I noticed almost immediately that there were more rules at Dad's. Mom had none. I did my homework, had a job, friends, didn't drink. Mom didn't need rules like a curfew or chore list. I came home before it was late and helped around the house without being told to. When I first told mom I liked Mike, mom had "the talk" with me, the birth control talk.

"I can take you to the doctor and we can get you put on something for birth control if you want," she'd offered.

"Mom! I'm not having sex!" I protested. We hadn't even kissed yet.

"I know, but you may change your mind, and if you change your mind at a certain time and place and aren't prepared…"

"Mom! I am not having sex, and I have no intention of having sex!" My face flushed. So embarrassing.

She'd dropped it and birth control hadn't been necessary. I didn't change my mind. I guess I was a prude.

I pretty much had no rules and had few boundaries at Mom's mainly because I didn't need them.

My Dad and Cheryl didn't know that about me. I mean, they really didn't know me well at all. Every other weekend and a month in the summer weren't the same as having someone live with you day to day. And Dad didn't work the same way Mom did. There was no loosey goosey with him. He had rules and curfews and boundaries galore. I didn't mind these at first, because I didn't have any friends and didn't really go anywhere, so what did it matter?

Things started out great. I got a killer summer job at Worlds of Fun, an amusement park in the city. I worked with hundreds of other teenagers at the funnest place in the city, and got paid for it. How cool is that? Every morning management had the "Operations" crew "test ride" the roller coasters to make sure they were functioning properly. We received free tickets and passes. I wore a cute little African safari outfit that made even me look hot, so it was all good.

Except for the puking. The cleaning up of puke was

the only downfall. We took turns dealing with that, so I only encountered it once a week or so.

There were tons of great people there and I made some friends I kept at arm's length. They were work friends and that was it. I chose to avoid the parties, just in case. All I wanted was to make a little money, have small talk with friendly people, and be able to just go home and not care too much about anyone else. It worked out well — a perfect time and place for me to heal, move on, and forget.

***

I kept busy and kept to myself. Forgetting.

Summer ended all too quickly. The school year rolled around and I started at Park High School. I got involved on the newspaper staff right away. I liked my classes and teachers. Things were good. Calm, boring, unemotional, so good.

I could even sit down in math to a clean desk with no pencil drawings on it. No smiley faces or notes from Mike on my desk. And when a guy came in and loudly dropped his books on the desk next to me and slid in his seat. I inhaled sharply. No empty desk beside me. I exhaled and realized it was a good thing.

Someone sitting beside me.

A clean desk.

A new start.

Panic attack averted.

Things were uneventful really. I went to work, I went to class, I went home. I had small talk conversations at all of those places. I didn't exactly experience incredible joy and happiness, but I didn't cry constantly either. I attended a new school with new people, and didn't have to pass the same row of lockers where Mike's and Julie's would haunt me. I kept busy, so I hardly thought of them at all. Doing that kept me at the highest pain free level I'd experienced since the accident. Everything was plain and ordinary.

~ ☾ ~

Until I saw *him*. As I walked to class in the basement by the theater, I saw a group of people sitting in the space under the stairs. They were clearly artsy types. The girls wore short, pleated skirts, with striped tights, and combat boots. They dressed the same way I had been the night I died, but they weren't going to a party. They just dressed like that on a normal school day. I envied them. I saw at least three of my cute hats among them, the hat which I hadn't had the guts to put on again since my drive to KC.

The boys were grunged out in torn jeans, heavy metal t-shirts, biker gloves with the fingers cut out of them. A bevy of activity and sound came off of them. They were right next to the classrooms by the theater so I had to guess they were theater kids. Every one of them sought attention, admiration, and validation from the others. They spoke to one another with big gestures and loud voices. They laughed big laughs and feigned shock and surprise at each other's stories. They were over the top, most of them.

One of the girls stood on the stairs as though she were performing to those on the floor. Clearly in the middle of a great story, she continued on her rant, and the others quieted to listen. A guy near the wall scooched down to lie on the floor with his head on his backpack, closing his eyes, not interested. One of the shorter girls who had crazy, wild, curly dark hair jumped up to add to the story, and the noise and activity erupted from all of them again, except the one sleeping in the corner.

But then there *he* was. He sat on the floor, his knees pulled up in front of him, hands casually resting on them. He wore ripped jeans, like the others, worn black Converse All Star sneakers, and an army flak jacket. He had dirty blond hair that hit his shoulders, tussled and random.

I couldn't see the color of his eyes, but he looked at

~ ☾ ~

me, locking on me and almost targeting me, like he'd found something he'd been searching for. His gaze didn't let up, and he watched me as I approached the stairs, carrying my books close to my chest. I glanced down, sort of embarrassed, as usual, my face blushing, but I could feel his eyes following me. The image burned in my brain. His stare and the slight smile on his face as he nodded absently while the girl with the crazy hair told some sort of dram-tastic tale. But his eyes were on me.

I'd walked past cute guys before. I'd had cute guys look at me before. But there was something about this brief moment in time that left a literal impression on my brain, some intensity or importance, some heat. Something about it, and I knew it would be a snap shot in my memories I'd never forget. I didn't know if I'd ever see him again, but the strength in that look touched something deep inside me. It touched my soul.

I continued to class and kept my head down. He was staring at me! That hot guy — no he's more than hot — that perfect boy with endless eyes was watching me. Wasn't he? No. That couldn't be. Full of yourself much? I figured it was nothing and hurried to beat the third period bell.

Life went on after "the look." I didn't know his name, and it didn't prompt me to do any investigative reporting on him. I didn't turn all stalker girl or anything. Besides, I probably just imagined him staring at me anyway.

"How is school going, honey?" Dad asked at dinner that night.

Family dinners were new and different for me too, where everyone sat and ate together, but this was important at Dad's.

"Fine." I took a large bite of mashed potatoes hoping to deflect a follow up question.

~ ☾ ~

Cheryl sighed, so I hurried through the bite and added some more for their benefit. "It's fine. It's a routine." I really didn't know what else to say.

"Do you miss your Mom's?" she asked.

"I miss my mom." I hadn't gone into the accident with them in depth. I didn't want to cry about it. I wanted to forget it. Cheryl didn't sigh again, and Sophie started talking about how the kindergarteners had caterpillars in class today, so I wolfed down dinner and holed up in my room for the rest of the night.

After the first few weeks of school, my newspaper advisor appointed us our beats and gave us our first assignments. We'd filled out a survey type questionnaire for her, and I guess since I'd written about going to plays with my Dad before, I was assigned the music and theater beat, which meant I would cover any assignments related to the choir or drama clubs, the school plays and that sort of thing. For my first assignment I thought I'd go get the scoop on the performing arts group. I spoke briefly with Mr. Black, the director, and he gave me a few names of students to talk to about it; one was his Teacher's Aide, Mo.

A nice guy with short, wavy, reddish hair, Mo sat forward eagerly on the edge of his chair in Mr. Black's office while I gave a quick interview. Almost immediately I recognized him from the hallway under the stairs as one of the theater types who'd been hanging around. *I wonder if he knows the guy in the flak jacket?*

"So how did you get involved in the show choir?" I asked though I really wanted to interrogate him about the perfect boy with the deep gaze.

He stared at me pretty intently, meeting my eyes so much it threw me off balance. I fumbled with my notepad and looked away, nervously. *Why is he staring at me like that?*

He wasn't a super attractive guy, physically, so I

thought I might be one of the few girls he ever talked to, he seemed so interested in the interview. Of course I might have been just being full of myself again. He could have just been a media hound. Whatever the reason, I got self-conscious and pushed on through the interview.

"Do I know you?" he asked, ignoring my initial question.

I paused and glanced at him. "Ummm, no, I just started here a few weeks ago."

"Oh." He looked confused and his left leg continued bouncing up and down. "You look really familiar."

"Umm, I don't think so."

"Ok, well, ah, after taking some of Mr. Black's choir classes I got interested in it. The group has auditions in the spring, so I tried out. I was glad the judges had no taste and let me in." He had a self-deprecating type of humor and made light of himself and his accomplishments. That went a long way with me.

"How long have you taken show choir courses?"

"Since junior high."

"What kind of stuff do you do? Like what's your specialty?"

"I act, sing and attempt to dance. Triple threat!" He smiled broadly.

"Since I wasn't here last year, what show did Park High put on?" I readied my pen.

"*Godspell* was our year end production." He grinned more to himself than to me, like there was some private joke.

"I think they tried to do that one at my old school, but the board wouldn't let them."

"It's good," was all he said, still grinning.

"And you were in it?" I pressed.

"Yes. I'm in most of the productions in one form or other."

Just then, the frazzled drama teacher stuck her head

into the classroom. She was thin, with an angular face, thick round glasses, and wild bottle blonde hair she'd tried to pin back from her face with little girl barrettes that had butterflies on them. She looked into Mr. Black's office where we were doing the interview and jumped back as though she'd seen a snake.

"Hey," Mo said, and waved at her.

She said nothing, but stepped out nervously, and hurried into the classroom where Mr. Black led the choir.

"Scary McNairy. She leads the drama side of the performing arts department," Mo explained.

"I could get a quote from her and ask her a few things then, maybe."

Mo clicked his teeth and sucked in air. "Ye-eah, I doubt it. She's not much for conversation. She's kind of a nervous Nelly."

"The drama teacher?"

"Weird, I know. She frightens easily."

"Okay then." I asked some more boring stuff for the paper and got some quotes from him, so he could see his name in print. After I thanked him and began gathering my things, he quickly added, "Hey, we're performing this weekend at the Ren Fest. You should come!"

"Ren Fest?" I had no clue.

"You've never been?" he practically gasped. "Awww, then you *have* to come. The Kansas City Renaissance Festival is amazing. People dress up in period costumes, they have period food, arts, jewelry, performances, jousting too!" He sat even further on the edge of his chair as he gestured madly. I thought he might fall off.

"Cool." I had nothing else going on and didn't have to work that weekend. "Sounds fun. I'm not sure how to get there."

He waved his hand at me as if to blow me off and shouted to Mr. Black, who was in the next room directing a choir. "Hey Black! Can ...I'm sorry I forgot your name."

"Lily."

"Lily." He said my name like it was a poem and grinned broadly before yelling back to Mr. Black in the next room. "Can Lily ride with us Saturday to do a story on the musical theater group?"

"Fine!" Mr. Black snapped sharply. I noticed Ms. McNair must have slipped out the side door because she was no longer there.

Mo didn't seem to care about disrupting Mr. Black's class. He simply turned back to me smiling. "There you go, you can ride with us."

"Musical theater group?" At the mention of the word *theater*, an image of a blond boy in an army flak jacket sitting outside the drama classrooms staring at me intensely popped into my head.

"Yeah this is a musical theater group, not just show choir. The music and theater departments are very close. We do a lot of things together and a lot of the students, like me, are in both, hence the creation of our group. We're doing several performances there. It'll be fun."

"Sounds great." I thanked him for his time.

The likelihood of flak jacket being in this musical theater group, just because he sat outside some theater classrooms once was slim to none. But I couldn't quit thinking about the possibility.

That weekend I climbed onto the school bus about to head to the Ren Fest, grateful I didn't have to spend my own gas money, and my heart skipped a beat when I saw him. Flak jacket sat in the back of the bus with some of the others I'd seen under the stairs. I self-consciously tucked my hair up behind my ear, glad I'd worn my cute hat for the first time this school year.

~ ☾ ~

4 At the Festival

The morning started off with a chill, so I put on my still new school jeans and optimistically grabbed a sweater I couldn't wait to wear, as I headed out. With the change of seasons, I could smell the crisp air on the edge of fall. The Kansas City Renaissance Festival ran for eight weekends in September and October, so the leaves changed into a multitude of colors, showing off with their reds and oranges and occasionally some purples, too. The sun was shining, so it proved to be a perfect day for some outdoor theater performances.

Nothing exciting happened on the twenty-minute bus ride. Mr. Black and Ms. McNair sat in the front seat. Mo sat with me close to the front and talked my ear off while I watched the scenery zip past us. I couldn't help but think of my past life with my lost friends. Having lived in a small town, Mike and Julie had never been to anything like this. We would have had so much fun. The familiar pang in my chest started to ache, and my hand rose to the scar on my forehead, healed now, four months after the accident, but I could still feel the raised line where the gash had been. If only my heart had healed by now.

I pushed the thought out of my head and focused on the now. I faced front most of the time, so I wondered who *flak jacket* had ended up sitting with, what *he* was doing, if *he* could see me from his seat, and if *he* couldn't, was *he* trying to?

Mo had described the festival perfectly to me. We poured off the buses and into the gates of the faux

~ ☾ ~

castles, and I let myself be carried away with the tide. Everyone walked around in Renaissance costumes, acting in character. There were harpists, jugglers, and costumed merchants hocking their wares. While it had been awhile since I cried about my friends, it had been longer since I'd felt happy. I hadn't been happy since before the accident, but here at least I could get lost in the fantasy and pretend I was somewhere else at another time, another person someplace long ago and far away. I went with it and escaped.

Mo led us to a circular stage with some canvas partitions which acted as the backstage area. Some already gathered in the audience. "I'm on after this first group," he explained. "Why don't you just put your stuff here and you can watch. Get some good pictures and all that."

"Make sure you get lots of me!" A tall girl with soft, corn silk blonde hair said, "I'm ready for my close up."

"Lily, this is Mya." Mo nodded in her direction. "She's shy." He smiled at her and rolled his eyes as he spoke.

"Yes, you all seem to be."

"Please," the girl with the long brown, crazy curly hair I'd seen talking to *him* weeks ago snapped. "Mya hogs the camera. She's always stealing focus!" This one didn't seem amused by the others. She had a pierced nose, cropped black leather jacket, pleated plaid skirt and tall, chunky boots. Oh, and my hat.

"You're just jealous." Mya pushed her playfully.

"Lily, meet Violet," Mo continued. Violet was shorter than Mya, and both were pretty, in different ways. Violet in a dark, wild way, and Mya in a more elegant, classic style. I just smiled a closed mouth smile at Violet and nodded politely. She didn't seem to be in the mood to make friends.

She glared at me. "Where did you get that hat?"

My hand self-consciously moved up to touch my hat

"Oh... uh... this? I got it a while ago." I tried to remember where, not that it mattered because it was a few hundred miles from Kansas City.

She nearly spat back. "Oh, this old thing? It's so five minutes ago," she mocked and moved to the opposite side of the partition to prepare.

Mo looked at me sympathetically, opening his mouth to say something, when *he* came up.

"Don't mind her. We don't." Flak jacket glanced in her direction.

My breath caught in my chest. I think I completely stopped breathing. When I realized I stopped, I quickly tried to start again. I'm pretty sure I looked like a total idiot. The blood rushed to my face at that realization, and I tried to shake it off immediately flipping through my story notes to look busy.

"I'm Luc." He smiled when I glanced up at him. People talk about love at first sight, and I had always thought it was a bunch of crap, but I got lost in his smile. There was something about him. He didn't smile, really. He had a certain kind of funny grin or a smirk. He was pleased with himself, I could tell. I could actually see those eyes this time. Green and deep. I could drown in those eyes. Confidence. He stood strong and tall. He didn't blink. He didn't look away. His eyes just pierced right through me to my core. Most of the people I knew at school would break eye contact out of insecurity or shyness or whatever. I tried to do just that, but I couldn't. It was like looking at a book I just couldn't put down. I had to keep reading because there was something more there, maybe something he was trying to tell me?

Mo bounded in between us and broke it up. Had he not done something, God knows how long I would have stood there, staring at this boy.

"Yes, thank you, Luc." He shoved him away and Luc

~ ☾ ~

dropped onto the bench next to me. With the eye contact broken, I couldn't get myself to look at him again for fear of being locked in Luc's gaze for the rest of the day. "Anyway..." Mo eyed Luc, clearly annoyed with him.

"Yo, losers!" A guy with long black hair pulled into a ponytail approached the group.

"And that's Sean," Mo explained. Sean's long hair could pass as Renaissance hair, but the black leather jacket and biker boots were a bit of a stretch.

"I'll be in the second set with Belle." Mo pointed over at a soft brown haired girl, noticeable for her perfect body. She wore a tank top that showed off her sculpted arms and flat stomach, and stretch yoga pants that highlighted her muscular legs. She waved and flashed a brilliant smile as she heard him introduce her, and took off her sneakers to replace them with calf high, leather boots.

"And..." Mo looked around. "Where the hell is Greg?"

Belle pointed behind the partition, so Mo jogged around the curtain to find him. "Oh for the love of.... Really?" He kicked something on the ground. I got up to see. Greg slept soundly against a barrel behind their changing area.

"Get up, Gregor!" Mo playfully kicked him again.

Groggily Gregor tried to protect himself. "What? Are we on?"

"Not yet! But—"

"Then what's the problem, man?" Gregor, aka Greg, had longish hair too, sort of like John Lennon. He wore round, blue tinted glasses and a tie-dyed shirt. I remembered he'd been the one sleeping on his backpack the first time I'd seen Luc under the stairway.

"Frustrating." Mo shook his head. "McNair and Black won't be happy about this."

At the mention of the teachers' names, I realized I hadn't seen much of them. They appeared to be just

~ ☾ ~

letting the students set everything up.

"Keep it down. Our audience is filtering in. We should get ready," Luc chastised him. I accidentally looked at him again, and he grinned back at me. Luc went to the backstage area for the performance, but from where I was sitting on the far end of the bench, I could see behind the partition. Luc reached over his head and grabbed his t-shirt from behind him, pulling it up and off. I tried not to drool and forced myself to look away. For being a grunged out guy who wore a loose old army jacket, Luc was in great shape. From the corner of my eye I could see as he pulled a ruffled front, loose fitting Renaissance shirt on over his head and wrapped a belt around his waist. I couldn't keep from looking back at him, now that I knew he was clothed. He kicked off his sneakers to put on his leather boots. He glanced up and caught me staring.

I quickly looked down to my notes and heat flushed my face again. After a minute, I tried to casually glance back.

The sun back lit him and shone through his hair. It made him look like the light came from him. It outlined him like some saint from a Renaissance painting I'd seen at the Nelson Art Gallery before. I stared at him like an idiot.

"So, Lily," Mo stepped in front of me and blocked my view. From the corner of my eye I could see Luc grin and turn away to get ready to go on. "Are you ready for the show?"

I didn't think anything could be as good as the show I'd just watched.

~ ☾ ~

5 The Performance

I sat near the front and took my camera out of its bag. I did my duty as the high school performing arts reporter. My Dad and Cheryl always took me to plays as a kid. Outdoor theater at Starlight in Kansas City and Broadway shows touring at the Mid Town Theater. I'd seen a few high school plays already at my old school, and they were okay. I prepared to take my photos, smile and look enthused whether I was or not. The actors were always nervous in the plays at my old school. Some of them swayed or shoved their hands in their pockets as though they just didn't know what to do with their own appendages anymore. They spoke in hard to hear shaky, low voices.

None of those things were happening with Mo and Luc's performance. Their performance played out like no high school production I'd seen. They oozed a cool confidence, smooth vocal control and body movements. No insecurity manifested. They projected in loud, clear tones. They didn't stutter over the Shakespearean language. They moved with assertiveness. They were unafraid of eye or physical contact. It was almost unnatural.

I couldn't believe what I saw at the Ren Fest. Mo, Luc, and Mya started with their scene from *Othello*. After watching Luc perform and barely being able to take my eyes off of him, I knew I was crushing in a bad way. But I liked Mo, too, with his enthusiastic and funny nature, and his genuine interest in staying on my radar and amusing me. Watching the two of them interact on stage

~ ☾ ~

as completely different characters, I couldn't believe I watched high school theater. How could their crazy, shy, nervous drama teacher could teach them that?

The following scenes involved the others I'd met — Sean, Greg, Violet, Belle — and were just as polished. The scenes fascinated me to the point I forgot to get photographs, so I hurriedly snapped some back stage after the show while they were still in costume.

Mo ran up to me as soon as they were finished. "Well?" he asked eagerly.

I smiled broadly. "I am.... amazed. Truly."

Laughing happily he hugged me and spun me around. "You liked?"

"I really did. That's the best high school performance I've ever seen." I even thought to myself it might have been one of the best performances of any kind I'd seen, including the professionals. It was just that good.

He stalled at releasing me after the spin. We just looked at each other, face to face, almost as if he were debating kissing me. I knew I wasn't ready for something like that and tried to figure out how to escape, when Luc came up behind him, patted his shoulder, and continued on his way. "Good job."

"You too!" Mo shouted after him, not taking his eyes off of me. But the interruption had broken our momentum, so he set me back on my feet.

Immediately, I started flipping through my notes, willing my face not to blush. "Yes, it was really great."

"I should get changed, and then we can check out the rest of the fest."

"Sure." I gathered my things and slipped back into press pass mode, observing and invisible, while he slipped backstage.

Violet got changed fairly quickly, and she and Mya seemed fine now. No fighting or hostility loomed over them from Violet's previous mood. Sean, however, came out agitated. He rummaged violently under the benches, grabbing people's coats and bags that were in the way and tossing them to the side, trying to find his wallet for a few minutes. He even sent a wood bench toppling over with a kick. I took that as a good reason to get off the bench I sat on and walk around to see if Mo had changed.

I turned the corner to the backstage area, to see Greg sleeping. *That'll make a good and apparently appropriate shot*, I thought, so I got my camera out and moved in a bit closer. He lay on his side, on the ground, already changed back into his Beatles style clothing with his head propped up on his duffle bag of costume clothes, quietly snoozing.

Then suddenly as I focused my camera on Gregor, angry voices erupted from backstage. Already in reporter mode, I tried to look invisible and inched closer.

"You can't!" Mo shouted.

"I feel it." Luc pounded his chest. .

I spied at them through a small gap between two curtains. I missed the beginning of Mo's response, but heard, "...came to me. It's mine, I'm telling you!"

"I don't know, man. I have to do what's right for everyone."

"This is. Trust me. I'm positive," Mo told him.

"For the others? For her?"

Mo nodded.

"You're one hundred percent sure?" Luc asked.

"A thousand."

"All right." Luc threw his hands up..

"Finally, after all this time." Mo put his hands together as if in prayer. "Thank God!"

"For the record, it's not an *it*. She's a *she*. I could swear I saw her before." Luc's voice trailed off as he emerged from the changing area and saw me. His eyes

~ ☾ ~

went right through me. "Hey there, Lily!" He spoke overly loud. His acting on stage had been much better than his attempt to warn Mo of my presence. Mo jogged up and peeked around Luc.

"Lily?" Mo's eyes widened. "How long have you..."

"Hey." I stood there behind the curtain like an idiot. Invisibility wasn't my forte apparently. I waved my camera and motioned toward Greg. "I got a great shot of your friend." *Please ignore me and look at Gregor.*

Luc glared at me, long and hard, as if he were attempting to read my mind. It took everything I had to look away and play dumb. Playing dumb *was* my forte, as it was pretty close to home most of the time.

"I got some great shots. I'm going to go take more around the festival. Wanna come?" I asked, to no one in particular. I hoped Luc would take the bait, but Mo came after me like a stray puppy. Luc didn't move but watched me intensely.

"Awesome!" Mo patted his jacket pockets, checking to make sure he had all of his things, did a final sweep of the backstage area and we were off. He didn't invite any of the others to go with us, and Luc released me from his death gaze and focused on tying his shoes.

~ ☾ ~

6 And the Beat Goes On

    I liked hanging around Mo, and he was good for the ego. I could see why he loved the Ren Fest. Musicians followed us along, piping their pipes, knights jousted in an arena up on the hill where a king commanded his champions to battle; boutique shops sold crystal necklaces, unicorn pendants and fairy bracelets. Incense wafted from some of the shops. I loved all of that stuff.
    We bumped into Mr. Black and Ms. McNair and some of the others throughout the rest of the day. While I was at a jewelry shop counter eyeing rings, Luc and Violet, or Vi as they tended to call her, came up. She chattered on and on about all of the ones she liked. It figured she did it for Luc's benefit, but he glanced in my direction.
    "Could I see this one?" I asked the clerk and pointed to a silver Irish Claddagh ring.
    The shopkeeper, outfitted in the Renaissance garb, which showed so much bosom it bordered on gross, accommodated me and brought it out of its glass case. I tried it on, holding my hand out to see how it looked on my finger.
    "It's beautiful, thank you," I told her while I slyly checked the price on the back of the ring. Gasp. I handed it back to her, and continued on my way, smiling at Luc as Vi bombarded him with her wish list.
    Mo had gotten us a table and some ginormous turkey legs to gnaw on.
    "I'll never be able to eat this in a million years!" I objected. He smiled and dug into his. Over lunch, I found out Mo was short for Monet, because his mother loved art.

~ ☾ ~

"What does she do?"

"Nothing." He quickly changed the subject, so I didn't press.

I tried to stay off the topic of Luc and focus on Mo. It sounded like they were fighting over me earlier, and Luc had given in. Clearly, he hadn't been that into me; I figured mainly because Luc was out of my league. I didn't have a chance, so I figured it best to avoid the chase, the rejection and the disappointment. It sounds horrible. Even though I was already butterflies crazy for Luc, Mo was funny and nice and already clearly into me. So I decided to try to set aside any developing feelings I may have had for Luc and give Mo a chance.

Mo made me laugh and I had a good time. Most importantly, he got my mind off of things. He got my number as we got off the bus, and life went on as it had.

The Ren Fest allowed me to escape to another time and place, to be another person. But reality hit me square in the face when I got back.

My first instinct when I got in my Citation parked at school was to call Julie and tell her everything that had happened. I even worried for a split second she'd be mad that I'd been hanging out with someone other than Mike. Then it hit me. Julie's dead. Mike's dead. I laughed. Not a lot, just a short laugh, because I thought to myself, *Well, I guess she won't' be mad then.*

Grief mixed with guilt. Guilt for laughing when I'd remembered they were dead. Guilt for having fun with other people. Guilt that I caused the accident because I'd opened the light up mirror, so Julie hadn't been able to see in the rain. Guilt for not staying dead with them, for surviving when they hadn't.

I couldn't help thinking about what their parents were going through, and the people who still sat on the other side of Mike's chair in math, even though there would be a new class and new seating arrangement by

~ ☾ ~

Speak of the Devil

now. There were those who stayed behind and me who left. I wondered if it would be easier there now, with the desks all mixed up. I kept thinking of the empty desk, but the students still there wouldn't see it anymore. Their lives were going on. Was it easier for them? Who was sitting in his desk now?

Panic gripped my heart as I wondered if the smiley face on my old desk had been erased or if it were still there.

I had left but my pain came with me.

~ ☾ ~

7 Anger

Mo phoned several times after that day, but I didn't take or return his calls. How dare I have a good day? How dare I have a good life when they couldn't? I caused the accident. I'd distracted Julie, and now she and Mike were dead but I lived. Dead. I should have celebrated the life I still had, celebrated the fact that I survived, but I just couldn't. Dead girl walking. That was me.

I wrote the Ren Fest story for the paper and got a B on it, but other than that, I wanted to bury that day like I'd buried my friends.

I didn't grasp the concept of time. *Time heals all wounds,* I thought over and over, hoping it would kick in. But I wasn't big on patience. *If I feel this way today, I will feel this way forever, right?* Love.... loss.... grief. Always.

But I'd left the accident behind, hadn't I? I'd run away from it. Maybe it was denial... a way for me to pretend none of it had happened. To pretend they were still alive and well somewhere. After all, I'd moved and there'd been no serious attempts from anyone else from that school to contact me. Granted I had refused to check any of my social media sites since the accident. I had no desire to hear news from anyone. But there had been no phone calls or emails from those I knew back at my old school. I didn't have any other friends really. This made it easier to live my life and imagine Mike and Julie still living theirs.

I pushed it to the back burner for a while. I had a new

~ ☾ ~

room at my dad's big house. I had a new school and a new job. I adjusted to my new family, so once again I kept busy. But in the quiet hours around dusk, after dinner and before bed, I was haunted.

Twilight, when the veils between the living and the dead are the thinnest, I thought, supposing it was something I'd read or seen in a movie somewhere. I don't know if I believed it, but something about the sun setting reminded me of them. Maybe I shifted focus from school to whatever else was happening that night at dusk, so my brain had a moment of down time. I'm not sure, but the pain always flooded in when the sun went down.

After being caught crying in my room by my stepmom a few times, I decided to suffer more privately. I didn't want to be fussed over. They couldn't help, and when they heard me, they just worried and tried to come up with solutions to my problem. Dad was big on things like solutions, goals, and the like. So my pain just worried them.

After dinner I went for walks. Dad's house was in a sub division which backed onto some woods and farms. He'd lived there since I was a little kid, and we knew the neighbors who owned the nearest farm. A gravel road ran along a barbed wire fence where some horses pastured. We used to visit there sometimes and we'd get to ride the horses for the afternoon. I walked there every day as the sun set and cried down an empty dirt road where no one could hear me but the horses. I did this for several days, but it didn't really help, and I'd return home hoarse.

After doing this for a week or so, I continued my walks but tried very hard to keep the crying to a minimum. I found beauty there. The dirt road curved through the trees that canopied overhead, and snaked off. Birds would sing. It made me think of some Emily

Dickinson poem we'd talked about in class. "Some keep the Sabbath going to church, I keep it staying at home." I wondered, if God was supposed to be everywhere, then surely He was on this road in the woods with me.

I must have been losing it, because I began talking to myself and to Him. As I watched the sun dip below the tree line and the sky turn all peachy orange, I asked, "Why did you take my friends?" Silence. "Why would you take such good, innocent, young people?" A bird chirped. "Why did this happen?" Silence again. "What is the point? Why did they get up every day, brush their teeth, study for geography tests, go jogging, have dreams of a future? What kind of sick joke is that?" A slight breeze blew through the leaves above. "What's the point?" More nothing.

I clenched my fists and stood up, searching into the treetops. "What is the point?" I yelled. Silence. The sun had dropped and the orange purpled and darkened, like a bruise forming.

I turned to walk home, my upper body stiff and my footsteps heavy, pounding the ground. "Maybe the point is there is no point."

"Lily." I turned at the sound of my name being carried on the breeze. But I didn't see anyone there.

I stared hard at the fence line and through the trees around me. "Who's there?"

No one answered. I knew I heard my name. Was it God talking to me? Yeah, right. Perfect. Not only am I sad, but I'm going crazy now, too.

I stormed home, bursting through the door and charging straight up to my room. Poor Owen shrank back against the wall to get out of my way.

Still fully clothed, I crawled into bed, unable to sleep for hours, but not worried about getting my necessary eight hours' worth. I mean, what was it necessary for anyway? It didn't matter. There was no point. I simply

~ ☾ ~

lay there, grinding my teeth and leaving marks from my fingernails in my palm from tightening my fists so hard.

While I hadn't been big on church, my mom and grandparents always had been. But now I knew for damn sure God was either indifferent or gone and, either way, I would never forgive Him.

~ ☾ ~

8 Spiral

    I would have prayed to God to bring them back, but He didn't care. I went through a period where I had faith when I was little. I believed, but after the accident, I needed to find my own answers. I'd been too young to have my family's beliefs forced upon me. Maybe at my age, people have to suffer the loss of a pet or a grandparent, but those deaths are at least expected. They fit in the life cycle. A dog only lives so long. A grandparent can only age so much.

    But losing someone my own age out of the blue, and not one, but two someones, it made me think, about life, about faith, about God. Things someone like me, who really just wanted to think about what to wear to school and whether I could pass that algebra test, wasn't equipped to deal with. It sounds strange, seeing as I'd had a "near death experience" as my mom and the preacher and the doctors had called it. Near death. There was nothing near about it. I had died, and when I'd told mom about the angel-like beings I'd seen, it just reaffirmed her faith in God and Heaven.

    But oddly enough, not me. I hit my head. I must have had a dream or a hallucination from brain trauma. If there were a God, why had he killed my friends? God didn't exist, or if He did, He was useless or careless or heartless. Frankly, I didn't know and I didn't care. There was no point.

    The harshest reality of all — there is no point. I realized at 16 that everything we learn, everything we attempt, everything we achieve is pointless.

~ ☾ ~

Speak of the Devil

I continued my nightly walks and turned this over and over in my head, night after night. Why? Maybe that's why religion exists. Thou shalt not kill. Thou shalt not steal. Thou shalt not whatever the hell else. In other words, don't steal my damned sheep or God will punish you many years from now in some afterlife. What a crock!

I must have been wearing my teeth down with all of the grinding I did lately. My muscles tensed as I thought of these things. My fists clenched. I thought moving away would make me forget, but living in a new city with no social life to speak of just gave me more time to think. With too much time and not enough to do, my mind went places probably best left alone.

It became more difficult to study because, what was the point? My grades reflected this. It became difficult to be kind to others... what was the point? I kept my family at a distance. If I got too close to them, well then who knows what might happen? I could lose them too. I let mom stay a few hours away. The distance seemed farther and farther away the less I returned her calls and letters.

I didn't care, and that became my new mantra. I think before it had been carpe diem, which you'd think would especially apply after the accident. But it changed, as did I. "I don't care." The apathy took hold of me like a disease, and didn't let go for quite some time.

~ ☾ ~

9 Don t Care

I tried to stop focusing on the accident. I mean, accidents happen, life sucks, no point, don't care. It had been five months since the accident. Autumn was in full swing. Halloween decorations were popping up all over and the stores were inundated with costumes and candy.

"Mo called the house for you again earlier," Owen said as I passed him in the entryway, emphasis on *again*. Since I wouldn't answer his calls on my cell, the one Dad replaced for me after my old one had drowned in the accident, Mo'd started calling our landline. How he got the number, I had no clue.

I shrugged.

"He's called you like forty-three times this week."

Usually I tried to speak as little as possible, to relate to others as little as possible, because… again, what was the point? But I stopped with one foot on the first stair going up to my room where I had hoped to retreat, conversation-less, and gave him a look. The apathy stare had formed naturally on me with no practice at all. My hair had grown too long in the front, because I wanted to hide the scar from the accident and I didn't care to get it cut, despite Cheryl's suggestions to do so, and it fell loosely across one eye, thus preventing me from having to make contact with *both* eyes, God or Bob or whoever forbid. Thus only one uncovered eye stared at him a beat, before he got another shrug with a "So?" on the side.

This was more conversation than we'd had in days, and Owen took it and ran. Owen my skinny, brace-faced

~ ☾ ~

brother at Park Middle School. He was a complete goofball, a nerdy eighth grader, and even though I wasn't like a cool kid or popular or anything, I was still a junior in high school. There was social credit in that, to a middle schooler anyway. I don't think any of that concerned him though. I think maybe he actually cared. The problem with isolating yourself because you don't want to deal with anyone is that it makes them wonder all the more what's going on with you, so you're approached even more than you would be normally.

"I don't know. Seems like you should call him back." He took a bite of the peanut butter sandwich he had in his hand, having just come from the kitchen to hijack me on the way up the stairs.

"What do you know about him?" I asked suspiciously.

He shrugged. "I don't know. I've seen him around." Mouth half full. Gross.

"Oh well, then, if you've seen him around...." Sarcasm. My weapon against the innocent. I turned and started up the stairs again.

"Lily." He never called me by name, so I stopped. He swallowed too big of a bite in a rush to communicate with me before I reached the top of the stairs, his hand going to his throat till the food was safely away. "I don't know what's going on with you. I just think..."

"Well don't." I didn't even turn around.

"I just think it might be good for you. You know, to go out and stuff."

I was difficult to get along with. I had gone through something I had a hard time dealing with and understanding, and he was younger and hadn't experienced anything like it. I could hear the worry in his voice. He cared about me, and a lump formed in my throat. A painful lump, which is the entire reason I was a recluse. I didn't want people to care about me, and I really didn't want to care about them. Yet here he was worried about me, and it made me choke up as though I'd been the one eating the peanut butter sandwich and trying to swallow the bites that were too big.

I started to say something but couldn't. I let my hair fall over my face and took off up the stairs, turning on apathy mode as I turned the corner.

Damn him for caring about me and making me care back.

I continued to wake up every morning and go to school. I wasn't a complete drama queen. I realized every time I felt sorry for myself for losing them, that other people had the right to feel a lot worse. So I went through the motions. School, work, sometimes homework. My priorities had shifted.

No, my priorities had just fallen by the wayside. I had none anymore. I didn't care about my grades. I didn't care about making friends. I functioned in survival mode. Eat, sleep, school… rinse and repeat.

Owen didn't exaggerate a whole lot when he said Mo had called forty-three times that week. I hadn't returned any of his calls. You know why. If I saw him at school, I ducked behind an open locker or down a side hall before he noticed me. I dodged him fairly well, but he became slightly stalkerish and all the more determined. My playing impossible to get must have done it for him. He became a man with a mission.

If he hung outside the newspaper classes, I'd wait for the bell and get a slip from Mrs. Madsen to go late to my next class, citing some delay in an article I wanted to finish up or some other lame excuse. She rarely noticed, being so stressed and busy. I avoided the drama and music rooms with a determination of a jewelry thief. If necessary I'd scale walls and drop down through ceilings to avoid him. I took the long way around the school to keep my distance, taking extra sets of stairs, back ways behind the gym, exiting side doors and returning

~ ☾ ~

Speak of the Devil

through the front doors, like I respected some restraining order.

But the school was only so big, and I couldn't hide like a ninja forever.

"Lily!" I heard him running up breathlessly behind me.

I stopped cold, hugging my books into my chest and closing my eyes tightly. "Crap!" I muttered.

The halls were clearing out. He caught me, took my arm and turned me around. "Lily!" His eyes searched for an expression or an answer. He seemed to want to say something else, but he just stared at me, bewildered.

I shrugged.

"What happened to you?" His hand still held my right arm.

"What? Nothing, why?"

"I don't know. You just look—" He stopped short, thought better of it, and went another direction. "I've been trying to get hold of you."

My mind wandered. I'd never done drugs, but I imagined the apathy thing probably felt almost like a drug. I didn't care about listening to other people and had no desire to rein in my attention span, so my mind would just go off on its own tangent, and I didn't care whether I heard what he said or not. It was trippy. At that moment, I realized what he saw.

He hadn't seen me since the Ren Fest trip a few weeks ago. Not up close anyway. That day I'd done my makeup, worn cute clothes and even my hat, and of course, curled my hair, which had been cut above my eyes. Today, in apathy mode, I didn't wear any make-up, my clothes were *probably* clean - no guarantees- but definitely not cute or accessorized, my hair probably needed to be washed yesterday, and it hung over my eyes. *Well, this should get rid of him then*, I thought. That thought made me start laughing.

~ ☾ ~

I realized how druggy I must seem and that made me laugh more at the ridiculousness of it. It reminded me of the car ride on the way to the funeral, where I knew how inappropriate and out of context this strange laughter was, but I couldn't stop. Then I thought of the funeral and laughing on the way, the tragic scene of Mike's mom there, and I laughed harder to keep from crying.

At least I don't think I cried. I meant to be laughing, but I couldn't be sure. Yup, this would definitely get rid of Mo.

He'd been talking about something while my mind had wandered, before the laughter but I hadn't caught it.

Then Luc came up with a concerned look on his face. "What the hell?" To the point. I stopped laughing and crying when I saw him, purely out of sheer terror, and just sat there in shock.

Mo shook his head, eyebrows raised.

"Come here." Luc took me by the hand and led me around the corner to a bench by the windows and sat me down.

"Luc, it's ok. I can handle this," Mo protested.

"Clearly," Luc said. And cue the butterflies. Sarcasm. Even in the midst of my emotional break I appreciated a man after my own heart.

"Luc!" Mo shouted.

Luc stood by me, unfazed. He reached in his pocket and flipped some money to Mo, who dropped half of the coins. "Go get her something to drink."

Mo, locked eyes with Luc for a second, jaw clenched, then sighed heavily, picked up the fallen change, and did as instructed.

"What's going on, Lily?" He looked me in the eye, probably trying to see if I was on something.

Oh God, don't look at me. I looked like hell right now, and the man of my dreams sat up close and personal. Apparently there were some things I still cared about. I

~ ☾ ~

shook my head, unable to speak coherently.

"Nothing? Nothing's going on?" He brushed my hair behind my ear, out of my eyes. I jerked back as though he'd burned me.

Then Violet skipped up and pounced next to Luc. "Hey Luc," She flirted, draping herself over the back of him. He pushed her away, gently but firmly.

"Not now, Vi."

She gave me one of those fleeting glances, then doubled back on me again. "What's with her...? Ewwww!" *Ha! I must look like total crap.* I almost slipped into nervous hysterics again.

"Violet!" he roared as Mo came running up. Mo pulled her back with one hand and gave me a Coke with the other. She stumbled backwards.

"Fine! Screw you guys!" she spat. Some of the others I'd met at the festival hurried by. Sean and Belle ran up, late for their classes but paused to look at me. They gave each other weird glances and Violet melded with them. They kept moving, on their way.

"Luc, I said I can handle it. Get to class." Mo clenched his teeth. I drank some Coke to make him feel better.

"Something's not right." Luc didn't take his eyes off mine. I think I felt another flutter in my stomach. Those eyes were crazy gorgeous.

"It's okay." I managed to get out, "I'm ok. Something just struck me as funny."

They glanced at each other, not buying it.

"Why haven't you called me back?" Mo asked.

"Mo," Luc reprimanded him.

"Well?" Mo went on.

"I've just been busy."

"For three weeks?"

Had it been that long?

"Mo," Luc said calmly. "I don't think this is about you or your phone calls."

~ ☾ ~

"I'm fine. Really. I just need to get more sleep." Probably somewhat true.

Luc took over. "Do you have a class right now?"

I nodded, unable to speak directly to Luc for whatever reason.

"Which one?"

"LA 3."

"With?" he continued, calmly, taking out a notepad from his flak jacket pocket.

I had to think a minute before it came to me. "Potter. Why?"

He pulled out a pen, jotted down something, tore off the top page of the pad, and handed it to Mo. "Take it for her," Luc said, pushing the paper down into his hand hard and glaring at him. Mo's shoulders slumped and he sighed again, not happy he'd been usurped.

"Now!" Luc told him. Without a pause, Mo turned and practically jogged to my next class, following orders. Whoa, that was weird, as though Mo had been outranked. I couldn't imagine Julie ever talking to me like that.

I turned to Luc, trying not to get lost in his gaze.

"You think Potter is going to take an admit slip from *you*?"

He smiled his mischievous smile and made me melt. "No, but he'll take one from Mr. Black whose initials I've perfected."

Luc was all kinds of awesome. How could I possibly be in apathy mode and be madly crushing on Luc?

~ ☾ ~

10 Breaking Down

What the hell is happening to me? Is this a nervous breakdown? Class wasn't really an option at that point. Mo had taken off toward English with a "note" for me. Good thing. Luc held out his hand to me and pulled me up.
"Let's go." He draped his arm around me to help me walk.
"I'm fine," I protested.
He just scoffed and walked on. Frankly, I liked his arm around my waist, so I didn't argue. He took me down the stairs at the end of the hall to the theater.
He opened the double doors to the house seating, but took me to the right, and directed me up some narrow almost ladder-like stairs which were painted the same reddish color as the walls. I'd never even noticed them before.
He followed me up. "This," he explained, "is the lighting booth."
I walked over to the window overlooking the house seating and the stage. "Oh." Brilliant conversationalist, I know.
"These are the switches for the stage and house lighting." He showed me the panels with glider switches on them and raised and lowered a few to demonstrate.
"Cool." I reached over to try a few for myself. He smiled and walked to the corner of the room where a bunch of pillows and even a sleeping bag were rolled up.
"This is also where we go when we aren't feeling up to classes." He sat down and patted the pillows next to

~ ☾ ~

him. Being kind of out of it and not exactly in my right mind, I just did as he directed. "You can stay here as long as you need to. You can think. You can sleep. You can study… whatever you want."

"I'll get caught." I never did anything like this. It never even occurred to me to skip classes.

"I'll cover for you. And if you did get caught…" he paused. "So what?"

So what indeed? He understood me, it seemed. I nodded. Maybe a nap would do me good.

"I'll leave you alone."

"No." I balled my hand into a fist to resist the urge to grab him by the pant leg as he stood up.

He turned back to me, eyebrows raised. "No?"

I tried to wave it off. "No, I don't know."

He took a deep breath, and I noticed his forearms tense. "You'll be fine." He glanced out the front windows of the booth. "I doubt you'll be alone for too long." And down he went.

God, I'm so stupid! I thought to myself. I practically mauled the poor guy. And with the whole laughing/crying bit. Geez, drama much? I felt like an idiot.

It was dim in the booth, so I lay down to try to nap, when I heard hushed voices coming from below. I crawled over to the ladder to listen.

"I'll take it from here." Mo sounded ticked.

"That's fine. I was going anyway."

"Good."

"I just want to make sure you have a plan here. That you know what you're doing." Luc crossed his arms, waiting for Mo's response.

"Dammit Luc, it's not your call!"

"I'm not saying it is, but if this is *it*, I want to make sure it's done right."

"What does that even mean?" Mo raised his voice.

~ ☾ ~

Speak of the Devil

Luc spoke softly. "You know damn well what it means. If she is yours, then it's down to you to fix it for her and yourself."

"Don't you think I know that?"

"Mo, seriously, I have no idea what you know."

There were some rustling sounds, like some contact between them. Then a thud as though someone had been pushed up against a door or a wall.

"Mo, you know what I mean. This isn't just about you. This could be big for all of us."

After a pause, Mo admitted, "I know."

Another pause. "There's something about her."

"She needs someone," Mo tried to deflect.

"She needs something, that's for sure. Let me know."

"I will," Mo answered. Then double doors at the front banged closed, and noise came up from the ladder.

Quickly, but silently, I crawled back to the pillows and feigned sleep. I heard Mo come up and sit nearby, but I didn't know what to say to him, so I kept my eyes closed. I tried to sort out what they'd said, and why they talked so strangely about me like I was a school project or some kind of petition drive. Whatever the reason, they were right about me. I needed something, and before long I fell into an actual sleep.

~ ☾ ~

11 Perchance to Dream

    I slept most of the day, waking occasionally to find Mo somewhere in the booth. Sometimes he lay next to me, other times he sat at the light panel reading textbooks. I would open my eyes, see him there, roll over and sleep some more. I hadn't been sleeping enough. My mind seemed to always be whirring about something. Sometimes I couldn't get the thought out of my head; I lived my life while my friends were dead. I'd worry I wasn't living it to its fullest and if I didn't that in some way I disrespected them. Other times I'd remember what it felt like when we died, the moment of impact, the car sideways as water rushed in, the pain, the inability to breathe, the cold and the blank. That would send me over the edge trying to think of something else... anything else, so I wouldn't remember our death repeatedly. It could sometimes take hours until I'd sleep. Then there were the times when I would imagine them in their coffins in the ground and wonder what level of decay their bodies were in. Had their coffin walls broken down yet, allowing bugs in to accost them?
    Morbid thoughts. Horrific. But these awful thoughts would worm their way in, and it took all of my strength to push them out long enough to get some peace and quiet in my head.
    Unfortunately when sleep would come, often so would the dreams. They weren't always horrible. Sometimes they were so happy and beautiful I'd wake up crying, realizing they weren't real. That I wasn't with Mike and Julie. That I was alone in bed and they were

~ ☾ ~

rotting in coffins and the worm thoughts would squirm back in and start the cycle all over.

Sometimes the dreams were dark. Sometimes we would be in math, the ceiling of the classroom would open up, and a dark cyclone would suck Julie and Mike up into the lightning swirls of the storm while I woke screaming.

There were others, too many to get into. Good, bad, traumatic. But today, probably due to the exhaustion after my emotional meltdown or the fact that I felt someone close by, someone who seemed to care about me, I don't know, but I slept in a much needed peace.

I stirred several hours later, to voices below again.

"Fine, I have to get to my last class anyway," Mo said.

"I thought she could use this," said a female voice I didn't recognize.

"Yeah, good," Mo snapped.

"What's she been doing?" I could hear concern in Luc's voice. What was with these musical theater types?

"Sleeping. The entire day away."

"She'll definitely need this then. I'm going up," the girl said.

I got up on my elbows as Belle's head popped up through the hole in the floor. She pushed a tray up before her and easily pulled herself up with her athletic arms as though she were doing a gymnastics maneuver. A tense silence could be felt coming from down below.

"Hey!" She smiled brightly. "I brought you something to eat."

I managed a half-smile sleepily while straining to eavesdrop on the whispers I heard below, but couldn't make anything out.

"I don't know if you remember me. I'm Belle." She brought over the tray of food from the cafeteria. She wore a matching yoga-like outfit. The yoga pants fit her snugly in all the right places. She pulled her hair back in a ponytail. I thought how perfect she'd be in an ad for something like probiotic yogurt or an energy drink.

"I remember. Thanks." I sat up, only realizing how my stomach growled when I saw the food.

"It's from the lunch room. Nothing major."

"No, it's great. I slept all day. Suddenly I'm starving. Thanks." Gratitude overkill flowed out of my awkwardness. Had she been one of the others who had seen me freaking out in the hall that morning? I couldn't remember.

She sat down on the pillows and beamed. She nearly glowed, she smiled brightly and with her perfect skin and shiny hair, it was a bit freaky, but I focused on the food and tried to keep my thoughts in line. One small thought at a time, or else they snowball out of control and go places I didn't want to go. I took a bite of the turkey club she'd gotten for me, when Luc climbed up the ladder and in the room. Perfect, me with no make-up and my hair all random and crazy, with a mouth full of food. Lovely.

"Hey sleepyhead," he said. A cutesy nickname. A thousand butterflies took flight inside me.

I held my hand up in front of my mouth, trying to chew this damn bite down and nodded. The bite took too long, so I just waved.

"Feeling better?" he asked. I nodded still chewing.

He smiled and those eyes... I tried to smooth my hair down. "Mo says you slept all day." He sort of said that as a question, too. Chew, dammit, chew. I nodded like an idiot.

"Give her a minute." Belle clearly felt my pain.

"Sorry. Mo had a class, so we thought we'd come check on you. Do you—" he started another question, but Belle put her hand on his arm. "Sorry."

After what seemed like a million hours, I swallowed and spoke. "No, yeah, it was good. I guess I haven't been sleeping much."

~ ☾ ~

"Really?" he asked. He probed for more information. It made me think of the way he and Mo had talked about me, even back at the Renaissance Festival. Like I was some school project or bet or mafia hit or fundraiser for a school trip. I got freaked out with their interest in me, so I didn't answer. He pursed his lips a bit and glanced at Belle.

"High school," Belle said, covering for me. "It's stressful."

"Yeah." I took a much smaller bite of a French fry this time.

"You didn't go here last year, did you?" she asked.

"No, I'm from a small town in the middle of the state."

"Oh, wow, this must be a lot to deal with for you," she said. When Belle talked she looked me in the eye, too. They all did, come to think of it. Sometimes people do that, but not like these theater types. They seemed to be looking into your soul, trying to read you or see something there.

"Ummm, yeah it is a bit."

"Is that why you're stressed and not sleeping?" Luc asked almost urgently. Belle again put her hand on him, and he deflated a bit.

"Uh, not really, no."

Luc turned away so I couldn't see his face. His body stiffened like he was mad at me. Belle kept her eyes on me.

"I'm sorry. I seem to be upsetting you," I said. He turned back to me all light and smiles.

"Noooo, why would you say that?" Belle asked, in her soothing voice.

"I don't know, he just seems..."

"Worried." He dropped the word like a lead weight.

"Ok, well don't." While I had feelings for him and wanted to be around him this entire thing was getting a

~ ☾ ~

bit strange, and as soon as people started worrying and caring, I figured I should just go. I took the bottle of water from the tray and stood up. "I gotta head out."

"No, you don't have to do that. If staying here makes you feel better—" Belle started.

"No, I should really go."

She protested, "But you've barely eaten anything!"

Luc stood and took my hands. "I'm sorry. Stay... a little longer."

I started to lose my breath at the warmth of his touch, or maybe my mind had rested enough to finally clear. "Why?" I asked, not wanting to pull away.

He paused. "Mo will be upset if you leave before he can see how you're doing."

The mention of Mo gave me the strength to pull back. "Why do you people care?" I started to get worked up.

"Lily," Belle started softly. "Something is going on with you, and we want to help you. That's all."

I looked to Luc for confirmation. He nodded his agreement.

"What are you, like, peer counselors?" I asked, half sarcastically.

Luc laughed, but Belle answered, "Something like that."

"We just want to help if we can," Luc said softly.

Belle stood up and led me to a chair. "We can refer you to Ms. McNair or one of the school counselors, but usually people are more comfortable talking to their friends."

"Friends?" I automatically went to Julie and Mike and a small town a few hundred miles away. Too bad for Belle and Luc, I wasn't much for subtlety. "My friends are dead."

12 TMI

There you have it. That shut them up for a bit, mouths hanging open, eyes wide. Neither of them looked quite as attractive and beaming as they had a minute ago.

"Yeah, so... my best friend and my kinda boyfriend were both killed in a car accident in May. I can't be fixed. Dead's dead." I had to say something.

They stared at me a little longer and then glanced at each other.

"I'm sorry, Lily. I'm just... at a loss," Belle said.

"*At a loss.* What an entirely appropriate phrase. It pretty much sums up how I've felt for like five months now," I told her.

More silence hung in the air. They weren't so great at this counselor stuff after all. Their silence started to embarrass me. So I rambled to fill it up.

"So there ya have it. Now you see. I'm not the best project for your little peer counseling group or whatever. I'm a mess and will be a mess until... well, until I'm not, I guess. So I'll just leave you to your next project." I took that as my cue to leave. You could cut the discomfort in the room with a spork.

I headed to the little trap door the ladder poked up through.

"Wait!" Luc nearly shouted at me.

"Look, there's nothing you can do—" I started.

"Tell us what happened." Belle quickly reprised her role as my therapist.

"I really don't want..."

~ ☾ ~

"Maybe talking about it will help." I think she knew it sounded weak as soon as she said it. I felt sorry for her so I tried to be merciful.

I simply answered, "No. It won't."

"Fair enough." Luc walked toward me. "But there must be something that will." I got stuck, looking him in the eyes. My breath caught in my chest and my muscles stiffened. He came to me and took my hands in his. They were so warm. Tingles ran up my arms and changed to butterflies. I thought I'd suffocate right there, standing in front of him, unable to breathe. Belle may have said something then, but I couldn't be sure. He pulled me towards him, and put his arms around me.

Normally I didn't get all touchy feely huggy. I found it weird even when even my own family hugged me and tried to avoid it as much as possible. I had thought it strange when Mike, who was almost my boyfriend, had done it, and pulled away. But this simple gesture, which appeared to be out of genuine concern and a desire to help when nothing else could, struck me. Since I could hardly move, paralyzed by his presence, I allowed myself to be vulnerable for once, allowed myself to be held, and in doing so I felt comfort and security like I'd never known. My mind raced and images of mountains speeding past as I soared above them, clouds, the sky, stars flashed before me. I felt like I was flying but unafraid, like I was perilously high above the earth, but safe. Like I was looking up into the heavens, and I felt it as though I'd been there before, like I'd done when I'd died with Julie and Mike. I almost felt like I could reach out and touch them. I remembered vividly the floaty white space and winged people. Suddenly I felt dead again. No, not the dead part, the after dead part. I felt the afterlife.

I jumped at the extreme reality of that … whatever it may have been, daydream.

~ ☾ ~

Luc pulled back. "What? What is it?"

I couldn't explain all that had just rushed through me, the images, the emotion. So

the flood gates broke and the waves rushed through me instead. I desperately tried not to cry. I fought the tears back with all I had but needed the release. Right then, I felt so safe and warm. My body shuddered and my face screwed up with the pain. Finally the tears came for several minutes, but Luc didn't push me away. He pulled me in closer and tightened his grip. He held me as though my life depended on it.

And who knows? Maybe it did.

Finally I stopped crying and had the decency to release him of my own accord. I had difficulty looking either of them in the eye. I was mortified, to tell the truth, but I didn't see a pixel of that reflected on him or Belle. She came over, stroked my hair back over my ears, and leaned in gently and kissed my cheek. Luc didn't let go of my hands.

"I'm sorry."

"You have nothing to be sorry for." Belle grabbed some napkins from the tray for me to wipe my eyes and nose.

I met their gaze to gauge how horrified I should be, but I didn't see judgment or awkwardness or anything I had expected in their eyes. In fact, they both looked as though they understood and empathized with me somehow. I swear I saw Belle nonchalantly dab at her eyes, and even Luc's seemed watery.

"I guess I needed to do that."

Somehow I let them pull me back to the pillows in the corner. "Tell us about it, if you can," Belle said.

"There's one thing I left out about the accident that killed my friends."

They waited for me to explain.

"I died in the accident, too."

~ ☾ ~

13 And Then Some

 Although I swore I wouldn't talk about them and focus on this death thing anymore, and even though I hadn't gone into it with my parents or Owen and especially not Sophie who was too little to understand, I found myself telling Luc and Belle the story of that night. The car swerving off the rain slick road, the impact, the darkness and dying, the fear and the peace, why I left, all of it.
 They listened quietly, glancing at each other every now and then. When I finished, Belle asked, "Do you believe in God?"
 I scoffed. "Don't get me started!"
 Luc smiled. "There's a lot of that going around."
 "Luc, don't." Belle chastised him.
 I didn't understand why she stopped him, but she went on. "I won't say something corny like 'They're in a better place' or 'They're with God now' but I can say your pain will ease with time."
 Geez, she sounded like a preacher. I laughed, unconvinced.
 "It will," she assured me. "It has to. Our brains are made this way for a purpose, so in time we forget the things that hurt us. Otherwise, we'd all go crazy." She smiled, half joking and I couldn't help but give her a little smile back probably because of the stress from the earlier breakdown and a glimmer of hope from getting rest or a relief from finally confiding in someone. But being with them made me feel better.
 "Someday, not today," she continued, "I want you to

~ ☾ ~

Speak of the Devil

tell me all about Mike and Julie more."

I nodded. "That would be nice."

"You're so strong, to have gone through that, to still be going through that." Belle put her hand on my shoulder.

"To have survived the accident and come back." Luc's voice faded off and he glanced away, lost in thought.

The bell rang, and I felt like they were surely thanking God for that.

"Eat this," Belle instructed as she went to start cleaning up. She handed me the sandwich, and again my stomach growled at the sight of it.

Soon after the bell, Mo came bounding up the ladder to the booth, panting like a giant puppy dog. "Hey! What'd I miss?"

The others I'd met at the Ren Fest, Greg, Sean, Mya, and Violet climbed through the trapdoor, too. Some others filtered in below on the stage. Their laughter wafted up to the booth.

The lighting booth started to get crowded with them all there. I stood like a stone angel, not wanting to explain everything again and definitely not with an audience. My face reddened as I remembered how these people who barely knew me had seen me break down in the hall. Luckily, the booth was dark and all of the light aimed at the stage where the other students congregated.

Violet hopped up on the counter, her short skirt baring crossed legs and tall over the knee socks. "Well?"

Belle saved me. "She woke up a little while ago and I'm trying to get her to eat something." I nodded dumbly.

Already bored with us she turned to the windows of the light booth to see the stage. "Ugh, look." Violet pointed to the others below, her face screwed up in disgust.

~ ☾ ~

Sean walked up to her. "*Ugh* is right. Why are they always grouped together like that?"

"Why are we?" Luc questioned him.

I stepped forward to see who they were talking about. A group of half a dozen or so students were on stage laughing, hugging, and paging through scripts. "Who are they?"

"Juniors," Violet spat.

"Oh," I laughed at that. "I'm a junior."

They looked at me aghast for a second, well, all except Luc who smirked, and then they burst out laughing.

"What?" I never seemed to get their jokes.

Mo came to my side and put an arm around me. "You're not like *them*; let's just put it that way."

Now I really wanted to know what they meant by that. I had a few classes with some of the juniors I could see below on the stage and tried to think of their names. A redhead with a pixie cut and dark, nerdy cool glasses named Cassie stood by the others and smiled at everything they were doing. Another named Kara with asymmetrical dark auburn hair who didn't stop moving, talking, singing, or acting held the stage. She was always on. A tall boy named Tim with spiky dirty blond hair with lightened tips and a clean cut look joined in with Kara for a bit, and then stood back to watch with Cassie. Hillary, a platinum blonde with wavy hair, could easily walk out the front doors today and get a modeling contract took the stage with them. A few others were with them on the edge of the stage, legs dangling over.

I started to ask what they meant. But Violet spoke up. "Auditions are coming up soon. They're practicing." Her eyes narrowed at the juniors.

"Rehearsing," Mya corrected. "You *practice* baseball. You *rehearse* theater."

"Whatevz!" Violet glared at her, tossing her crazy curls over her shoulder in response.

~ ☾ ~

"You should try out," Mo said to me.

"What? Are you crazy?"

"Why not?"

"You forget. I've seen you guys perform. There's no way I could compete."

"Doesn't hurt to try," Belle said. "Acting is fun. It gets your mind off real life." She gave me a knowing glance.

"Which must be why they're here," Sean said, still glaring at the juniors.

"They're so happy it's just gross." Violet tucked a rogue strand of spiral curl behind her ear.

In watching them, I had to agree. They seemed really happy. I glanced around the booth at the seniors here. Greg had taken up my spot in the corner by the pillows, still wearing his John Lennon round glasses, though his eyes were already closed. Violet and Sean just looked pissed. Come to think of it, they had been every time I'd seen them. Mya rummaged through her purse. Luc and Belle had just been put through the emotional wringer and were trying to cover with a feigned, everything-is-okay face. But when I looked to Mo, he just stared at me, like he hadn't noticed the others, like no one else even existed. Like I felt with Luc, how I couldn't look away.

He frowned after our eyes met. "Is everything okay now? You look…"

"Yeah," I started.

Luc finished. "I'll catch you up later. I think Lily was just heading home. Are you good to drive, Lily? Do you need a ride?"

"Oh, yeah, I'll be fine."

"Someone can go with you if you want," he added. I was clueless as usual. I didn't know if it was a hint he wanted to go with me or if he wanted to pawn me off on Mo, or if he just wanted me to get the hell out. Before I could process a response…

"She said she's fine. God!" Violet snapped. "We have

~ ☾ ~

to rehearse! Someone read lines with me." She latched on to Luc's arm, pulling him toward her.

"I'll walk you out," Mo said, before Luc could offer any more help. Mo put his arm around me, turning me away from them and started guiding me out. I wiggled free to turn back to Luc and Belle.

"Thanks... both of you. I really appreciate it."

"Sure thing!" Belle chirped happily before eating the rest of my fries.

Luc just smiled, sort of sadly as I left, Violet babbling in his ear.

Mo went down the ladder, holding my waist to help me down. "What'd they do?"

"Oh, we just talked."

"About what?" he asked, a touch of suspicion in his voice.

"Stuff." I couldn't get into it again.

"Oh." An awkward silence settled around us like a heavy fog as we walked to my locker. "Listen, Lily. I'm having a Halloween party this weekend at my house. Will you come?"

"This weekend? Like costumes and stuff?"

"Yeah Friday... till whenever." He grinned.

I didn't have to work, and I liked this group, well most of them. Violet acted like a bitch most of the time.

"Yeah that sounds good." We arrived at my locker.

"Yeah?"

"Yeah," I smiled at him.

"Well, I was sort of asking... I guess I didn't do it right. Or maybe I did." He fidgeted with his hands and couldn't make eye contact. I thought his nervousness was very charming, especially since he didn't get nervous on stage. "I sort of wanted you to go with me... as my date."

I smiled. "You sort of wanted me to be your date?"

"Well no, I *really* wanted you to be my date." He

~ ☾ ~

looked at me with his blue eyes. They were innocent and puppy-like, but I knew from the conversations I'd heard and the strange interactions he and his friends had with one another that I didn't yet know the whole story about him or the others. For whatever reason, I wanted to find out more.

With a glance back toward the theater, memories of Violet draped on Luc, and the conversations I'd overheard where Luc had basically retreated when the topic of me had come up, I decided to let the fantasy of Luc and me go.

"Sure," I agreed. He beamed and started sort of bouncing up and down on the balls of his feet excitedly, which made me laugh.

"Great! I'll see you tomorrow and we'll work out the details. That is if you aren't going to be dodging me anymore." He didn't stop grinning.

"You'll see me tomorrow."

"Great!" he said again, bounding off down the hall back to the theater. He reminded me of Dusty back home. Like a big dog that thinks he's a little puppy. I grinned, filling my backpack up with books, guessing at what homework I'd missed that day. I figured I'd check the class websites at home and hope the teachers actually updated them for once.

I felt much better as I headed to my car. The theater was right by the back doors of the school which led out to the parking lot, so as I walked by it on my way out I decided I would peek in on them a little to see them practicing or rehearsing or whatever they were doing. I didn't want to talk to anyone or be seen, I just wanted to watch for a little bit. I went down the side hall next to the theater, which had a single door that opened in on the house seating and was close to the stage. I put my backpack down and carefully pulled the door open a crack, so I could see in.

~ ☾ ~

The juniors had been shifted from the stage down to the house seats. Some looked a little grumpy about this. Spiky haired Tim sat, arms folded across his body, while Kara stood hands on her hips and her back to the stage, in protest. Most of the seniors were on stage, although I couldn't see Luc or Mo. "Guys! Seriously!" Violet shouted as something offstage broke her concentration. She glared over her shoulder to the backstage area. "Take it outside! Luc!" She sighed, heavily, shook her head and tried to continue, script in hand.

The reporter instinct in me kicked in, and I just had to know the whole story. I crept to the next single door down the hall alongside the theater, which led to the backstage area. I didn't have to open it. I just had to listen. I could hear them shouting before I got there.

"I leave you for five seconds and you're making a move on her!" Mo shouted.

"It wasn't like that, Mo. She needed someone and you weren't there," Luc replied.

"And why was that? Hmmm? You told me to go to class and give her some time. You were just getting rid of me so you could move in."

"Look, again, you seem to think she's yours…"

"She came to me!" Mo roared. "First contact was her coming to me for the article she was working on."

"There's something more to it. I can't put my finger on it. I know I saw her before…" My mind immediately went to Luc sitting under the stairs as I walked by at the beginning of the year. His eyes locking on mine. Was he trying to remember that moment?

"There's nothing more to talk about. It's a done deal. I'll take care of it. She's with me. She's coming to my party Friday with me!"

"Does *she* know?"

"Screw you!" I heard hard footsteps going up stairs, probably to the stage. I thought I should head out.

~ ☾ ~

Speak of the Devil

What was with them? Guys weren't breaking down my door or anything. I certainly wasn't as attractive as Mya or Violet or even some of the other theater junior girls in there. Why did they have this territorial tendency and why did they keep claiming who I did or didn't belong to? Bizarre. I started regretting accepting his date, but blamed myself. The conversation I'd just heard wasn't for me to hear. I should put it out of my head and continue on as though it never happened.

That was the plan. I hurried off past the theater and to my car, hoping not to be seen.

~ ☾ ~

14 Fallin

 Although some of their conversations were odd to say the least, I liked being a part of them, being a part of anything really. At Blair High School the only thing I'd really been a part of was the trio with Mike and Julie. I wasn't popular or anything. Park High had close to 1,000 students and me being so new, I couldn't have told you where the in crowd lunch table even was. Maybe they didn't have one. What kind of teenage dream would that be?
 Yet I had come here to run away and hide my head in the sand, and that had been something I'd done quite well. But all of the hiding and not talking to my family and not really having anything beyond small-talk friends... I needed to be around people, to talk with someone. For whatever reason, these theater types seemed genuinely interested in me — almost too interested. Still, the only other thing on my plate currently was not caring about school or wallowing in grief, so I figured I'd just go with it.
 I had always been a rule follower, someone who had worked out pros and cons of doing something, going with what made sense. None of this did, but having shifted to the 'I don't care' method, I figured I'd just go with the flow and see where it took me. I guess it all boiled down to I didn't care if it worked out or not. I'd still be me. My friends would still be dead. Something else would come along.
 I told myself those things anyway, sitting on my bed listening to Jimmy Eat World on the radio, half-

~ ☾ ~

Speak of the Devil

heartedly doing homework. I got a picture of Luc in my mind and his intense eyes and the sparks I felt when he took my hands in his. I'd shake it off and turn up my radio a little louder to drown out the image. I tried to think of Mo, his smile, his enthusiasm. He seemed so happy I'd accepted his date request. I liked seeing someone happy. I was jealous, not having allowed myself to feel that way for a while except in short bits.

    Maybe Mo reminded me a little of Mike. Mike had always been happy like that and excited to see me, almost puppy-like, too. Why did I always have to do that? I always went back to Julie and Mike. I thought of what Belle had said; it would take time and eventually hurt less, but how long would it take for me to stop going there?

    Since my eavesdropping a few days ago, Luc made himself scarce, and Mo had done the opposite, hanging out before school waiting to walk me to my first class, hanging around after to walk me to my car, sitting with me at lunch. It didn't bother me. I missed Luc though. He'd helped me so much just talking to him, and when he held me... It sounds stupid, but it was powerful or magical. The warmth just, I don't know, helped me... made me feel better... healed me. Weird, anyway, and now I never saw him. Mo seemed fine and perfectly happy not to mention Luc or his whereabouts. Had I not heard their blow up I probably would have asked about Luc, but knowing they'd fallen out over me, I thought it best not to. I questioned whether I should or if it would be obvious I knew something, and I'd second guess myself right out of saying anything and the moment would pass.

    I really missed Luc. Sad but true. Like I was just meant to be around him. I know about simple attraction, but it was more than that. When I woke up in the morning, my first thought was of him and how I hoped I'd get to see him that day. Whether I actually did or not determined whether it was a good day or bad day. At night I fell asleep thinking about him and hoping I'd dream about him at night. I felt a physical need, a hunger to be with him. With Mike and Julie, I always had them so the need never overcame me, but I always just knew I belonged there with them. This need for Luc started to worry me. It wasn't normal for me and didn't seem normal for anyone else I'd ever talked to about this sort of thing.

Was it a crush? Was I hanging out with Mo in order to be near Luc? No, I liked Mo, too, just in a different way. I felt good around Mo. But I needed and wanted to be around Luc. It would cause too much friction between the two of them if I flip-flopped now. Bottom line, did I really care anyway? Everything was temporary, so why sweat it? I just went with it to see what would happen at the party and waited for the weekend.

Family — unavoidable.

School — uninspiring.

Work — uneventful.

If nothing else I kept my mind occupied wondering if Luc would be there, who else would be there, what a date with Mo would be like, what they would be dressed as.

Crap. I need to find a costume.

15 Par-tay

    Mo bounced around me all day Friday, his usual, giddy self, but he didn't meet my eyes as much as usual. The thing with these theater types was they were so self-confident. When I'd seen them perform at the Ren Fest their self-assurance had made their performance stand out above all of the other high school performances I'd seen. They had zero inhibitions. I'd been watching rehearsals for the last few days, too, and there were no cracks in the facade. I envied that. Even the dreaded juniors oozed this complete state of self-actualization. I couldn't believe it. I decided Ms. McNair must be an extremely talented drama teacher and thought I'd like to sit in on a class and do a story on her.

    When I mentioned it to Mo, he deterred me. "She's never there."

    "What do you mean?"

    "She goes out on leave a lot."

    "So, who teaches you?"

    "A sub."

    "Is *she* a good teacher?" I pressed.

    "No, it's an old guy who sits and does crossword puzzles the whole time and yells at us to be quiet every five minutes."

    He didn't really know why or where Ms. McNair went, just that she was never there. How they all got to be this good was beyond me.

    Whenever I'd drop in, if Luc were on stage, he'd disappear as soon as he noticed me. I caught nothing but glimpses of him, and Mo would be with me,

~ ☾ ~

distracting me before I could think much of it.

I knew he'd be at Mo's party though, so I panicked over what to dress as. Mya and Violet always wore the cutest outfits, and could easily pull off a sexy costume, something I'd always been too shy to wear for fear of being made fun of. Small schools do that to you. I never wanted to stand out too much, but here, I had to stand out or everyone would pass me by. I needed to take more risks with what I wore at this school, but they were baby steps.

I figured I could go as a dead girl, but would that be in poor taste? I mean, if so, the only person I could offend would be myself. But dead girls weren't attractive, so I decided to go as a cute witch. When I went to the store I found lots of sexy witch costumes with skimpy black dresses, fishnets, long black gloves and black feathery hats, and traditional scary witches, but also came across Glinda, the Good Witch from the Wizard of Oz and went with that instead. It came with a crown, a big poufy princess gown, and gossamer fairy wings. I raided Cheryl's closet and found some white lacy heels she'd worn to a party years ago, and they went perfectly with the ensemble. I added some sparkly eye shadow, some fake eyelashes, dusty rose blush and light pink lipstick and was ready to go. If only I had a giant bubble to float in on.

"Pretty." Sophie watched as I did the finishing touches to my make-up.

"Oh hey!" I hadn't noticed her there watching. It was cute she did that when I was getting ready, and it made me feel kind of pretty.

Owen stepped up beside her. "You seem nervous for someone who doesn't care at all." He grinned.

Another one with a bit too much self-confidence. "What do you know, maggot?" I replied, pushing past them to finish up in my room with the door closed.

~ ☾ ~

"Hey! That's not very good witchy sounding. Get in character!" He snorted. Brothers.

Since Mo was busy getting everything ready for the party at his place, he asked me to drive myself. That worked for me. The awkward meeting at my door would have been... well, awkward. I didn't mind avoiding that. Of course, we'd have to have an awkward meeting at his door, but I didn't think that far ahead.

I'd driven by the outside of his place before, so I found it easy enough. I'd never been inside, though. I heard the Foo Fighters playing on the stereo as I came up to the door. I wondered if Mo's mom was home. My Dad and Cheryl would never let me have a party without being there. Mo was a senior though, so maybe a shift was coming.

The outside wasn't decorated much for Halloween save for a cardstock black cat taped to the front door. Inside I could see orange and black balloons and some streamers, but nothing major.

I knocked, but no one could possibly hear me over the music. I opened the door, cautiously peeking in. Impressive. The place was packed and everyone had costumes on. I thought he had a pretty tight knit group, but apparently he had more friends than I knew about. I instantly worried he may have posted about his party on Facebook or Twitter and then realized I didn't even know if he had Facebook. Oh God, what if this was some Project X type of party. If it got crazy, I would take off. I had no trouble abandoning wild parties. I knew not to drink and drive.

I closed the door behind me and walked in. Mo lived in a traditional split-level ranch. To the right were stairs going up, to the left was a more formal living room / dining room area that circled around to the kitchen straight ahead. Between the kitchen and stairs going up, another set of stairs headed down. Mo lived in a pretty

~ ☾ ~

modest house compared to my dad's. This was middle class at best, but nicer than my mom's old farmhouse.

Mo lived with his single mom, so obviously they had one income to keep them afloat. He never talked about his dad, so I didn't know if he helped them out or not. As I pondered these things, I saw her, the woman who must be his mom, sitting ahead at the kitchen table and smoking. Ugh, I hated smoke. I headed that way, but she didn't appear very approachable. Lines lay heavy on her face and around her mouth, as she sat staring out the window, oblivious to the party around her. She had short dark, stringy hair streaked with gray, and a hard looking face with vacant eyes. She wore what I'd call inappropriate clothing for a woman her age, a spaghetti string tank top with no bra, shorts and tube socks. The insufficient amount of clothing revealed her stick thin frame. She was definitely no MILF sitting there half naked. She looked old and drawn with unhealthy skin. She just stared almost unaware of the noise around her.

I felt awkward, like I should introduce myself. All of the partiers around her acted like she didn't even exist, grabbing beer from the fridge, mixing drinks, and leaving without fear of chastisement for underage drinking. She continued to gaze out the window, and I found myself staring at her. People moved between us, in and out, while the music swelled, and I watched her from about 15 feet away, between the kitchen and entryway, trying to figure out if something was wrong with her or what. Suddenly she turned from the window, eyes blazing at me as if she'd heard my thoughts. Her eyes narrowed at me, hard and hateful, making me jump.

I turned to run out the door thinking, *Screw this noise*, but slammed right into a Navy Seal. Luc. He had donned camos, black combat boots, a black vest with a patch that said "Navy Seal" for those too slow to figure it out. He had a holster strapped to his thigh and some

~ ☾ ~

other military items hanging from his belt, and wore a black cap and dark sunglasses and carried a fake gun. Man, that costume was hot.

I started to apologize to him for bumping into him but he stood there, his mouth hanging open, so I didn't know what to say. I glanced away self-conscious of my ginormous poufy dress and wished I could click my heels and disappear.

"Wow. You... look... amazing." His eyes were wide.

"Oh, thanks."

"Angelic even. Just... I don't know. It suits you."

"Thanks." Yup, me and my mad conversational skills.

"Where were you going?" he asked and that snapped me back to Mo's mom. What the hell? Was she trying to be scary for Halloween or what?

"I don't know, I..." I turned to point her out, her meanness, her cold stare, but when I did she faced out the window again, the ash at the end of her cigarette, now longer than the cigarette itself, curled down without her attention.

"Don't worry about her." He offered no further explanation. I relaxed with Luc next to me. He put an arm around me, careful not to bend my wings, and comforted me. I felt the heat through my gown, relieved to see him again, to feel his touch again, but I knew it had to be handled carefully. Mo had invited me here as his date.

"Come on, he's downstairs." Like he read my mind. I avoided taking one last look at Mo's creepy mom.

I think Luc knew he shouldn't be off with me alone for too long. His arm went to the small of my back as he guided me down the stairs. I tried to ignore the sparks that shot through me at his touch.

Mo stood at the bottom of the stairs dressed as a vampire and talking to some people who were sitting around watching a movie.

~ ☾ ~

"Heeeyyyy!" Happy as usual. "There she is!" He paused eyeing my costume then started laughing. I noticed him glance at Luc and for a second I thought he'd be upset Luc had walked me in, but he motioned at me and said, "Did you get a load of this?" Luc nodded and smirked. "Wings and everything!"

Instant self-consciousness overcame me. I looked away and tried to smooth my poufy dress down some.

"No, no, no!" He took my hand. "You look beautiful!" He pulled me closer to him and away from Luc who disappeared way too quickly, the warmth from his hand dissipating instantly. Mo introduced me to several people who I soon forgot and went to get me a drink.

"A Diet Coke or water is fine," I called out to Mo as he bounded up the stairs, his cheap vampire cape flapping behind him.

"Diet Coke?" Belle sounded a bit disappointed as she came up to me in her blue fairy costume. I hadn't seen her when I came in. "It's a party, Lily!" She draped an arm around me as she slurred her words. "You look pretty. Oh! I have wings, too!" Drunk already. My heart sank.

"Hi Belle."

"Hi yourself!" She stumbled, fell into me, and laughed. This wasn't the thoughtful, kind girl who had helped me earlier this week. My muscles tensed. I hated things like this. I hated the drinking. I hated seeing her turn from being so cool and caring into this. I started to squirm and fidget, and for the second time in the few minutes I'd been there, I considered making a dash for the door.

But once again, out of nowhere, Luc appeared positioning himself between me and the steps. His shades were tucked inside his vest pocket, and his eyes were clear and bright, although he held a beer. I got stuck in them as usual and immediately felt at ease. I

~ ☾ ~

glanced around, and realized very few people were already in the drunken state that Belle was. She finished off her drink, staggering away from me toward a bottle of wine abandoned on the coffee table. She picked it up and started drinking straight from the bottle on her way upstairs. I think she'd forgotten she'd been talking to me at all.

This left me with Luc again and a room full of others I didn't really know who were watching the movie. "You look really nice," he said.

"Oh, thanks. This old thing?"

His smile lit up the room.

Suddenly Mo bounded down the stairs and came between us, Diet Coke in hand. "For the fairy printheth." He lisped through the fake fangs.

"Glinda the Good Witch... you know from The Wizard of Oz."

"Oh, right. Nithe. Damn thethe thingth." And he took them out so he could talk and drink.

"Wow, you have a great turn out!" I shouted over the noise.

"Yeah, not bad." He took a sip of his beer, but like Luc, you wouldn't have known it. They were both unaffected. That's what I do, make reporter like observations at parties. Cool, I know.

"I think I saw your mom." I gestured up the stairs.

"Yeah? She's around somewhere."

"She doesn't care? That you're having a party?"

"Psssh, no. She doesn't care" His eye clouded over, and he set his jaw like he was grinding his teeth.

I figured now wasn't the time to ask about his dad, so I just looked to see what they were all watching and what they could hardly hear over the music from upstairs. *Ghostbusters*.

At one time or other, I saw the rest of his friends and a few of the juniors from the theater around. The juniors didn't associate with Mo and his friends much, but they were there. Tim was in a Jedi costume, Cassie, who I realized looked like that red-headed girl from all of those John Hughes movies from the 80's, was dressed as the Mad Hatter, and Hillary, who liked like a real life Barbie doll was dressed in the sexy witch costume I came close to buying. I breathed a sigh of relief I hadn't. They kept to themselves, playing cards with each other, and looking around, appearing a little on edge.

Someone in a Scream costume was lounging in a beanbag chair in the corner and seemed to be watching a movie until he rolled over on his side as if he was asleep. "Oh my God." I pointed at him. "Is that—?"

"Gregor."

"How can he sleep with this noise?"

"Greg can sleep anywhere. It's a gift," Mo said.

Luc had vanished again, somehow unnoticed by me. I could hear Violet's piercing laughter coming from upstairs.

"You seem tense."

"Yeah, parties aren't really my thing."

"Mo!" someone shouted from upstairs.

"What?" he shouted back, annoyed.

"You gotta get up here!"

He apologized to me and took off up the stairs, taking them three at a time. I settled into a love seat in front of the movie with the others who watched zombie-like, sort of like Mo's mom had been acting, and decided to people watch.

I wondered how Mo knew all of these people, and if I looked as out of place as I felt. I decided to pretend to be fascinated by the movie, so I wouldn't look like I'd been dumped here alone.

I fidgeted with my hair and my wand and didn't really know what to do with myself. I didn't know how the whole dating scene worked, how we were supposed to be

~ ☾ ~

Speak of the Devil

acting with each other, whether this was a real date or what. His mom was upstairs. Minors were drinking. I tried to process every aspect of this night, and come to grips with it. Maybe we should have gone on a regular date, dinner and a movie and a kiss goodnight — something safe and conservative. Drunken party first dates... not really a great idea.

"Sean got into a fight." Luc appeared, startling me. "Sorry. Mo is dealing with it."

"Is everyone ok?"

"Yeah. It happens on a pretty regular basis, especially in situations like this."

Luc sat down next to me. Right there close enough to reach out to and touch. My heart raced. Other than leaving this party as quickly as possible, the one thing I wanted more than anything else was to kiss Luc, to lean in and feel the warmth of his lips, the closeness. It would be so easy, too. He sat right next to me, his eyes scanning the room intensely, like he needed to be on guard or patrolling. What was it about him? Maybe he was in character? Wisdom colored his eyes, like he was older by more than just a year. He had a protective quality to him, like he waited for something to happen and knew he needed to be ready. And there was a light... I couldn't quite explain it, but an aura surrounded him. I didn't totally believe in all of that, but I definitely sensed goodness in him, purity. I don't know but something about him just radiated, a presence, a vibe. I couldn't put my finger on it, but in those few seconds of watching him, and not being held captive in a locked glance with him, I started to see him. Really *see* him and understand something. He turned and met my gaze.

Breathe, Lily, I thought. Breathe or you will pass out.

"I need some air." I stood to go before I did something completely stupid.

"Are you okay?"

~ ☾ ~

"Fine." I didn't let him block my escape this time. I wound my way through the others, up the stairs and toward the front door, not looking in the kitchen for Mo's weird mother. Out of the corner of my eye I saw Mya dressed as a monster bride, dabbing at the side of Sean's mouth with something and Mo hovering nearby. I didn't make eye contact but kept going.

Keep moving, Lily. Out the front door to the yard. Go. The noise from the party muffled as the front door closed behind me, and the cool air helped clear my head. I looked down the street to my parked car and made the decision to leave.

Behind me the door to the house opened. "Lily?"

Keep walking, I told myself, but my body didn't listen. I turned back around to Mo.

"Where are you going?"

"I just needed some air."

"Here. Sit down."

He came up and put his arm around me, and the warmth from him helped me relax. "I'm sorry. Parties just aren't really my thing," I repeated.

He smiled. "You said. They aren't exactly conducive to conversation really."

"No." I smiled now, disarmed.

"It's ok. We can do whatever you want to." He brushed my hair back out of my face. "You are so pretty. No, more than pretty. Pretty doesn't do you justice. Beautiful works maybe."

I could feel the blood rush to my face and couldn't keep the smile hidden. I started to question whether Mike had ever told me that, and then Mo leaned in and kissed me softly on the lips. For once, my mind stopped and didn't go there, to the dark, sad place of loss and death. I decided to go with the now and live in the present rather than mourn the past or worry about the future.

~ ☾ ~

While there were no sparks or butterflies, there was warmth. My mouth returned the kiss, pressing against his lips. He kissed me with gentleness, sweetness. I felt kindness in this kiss, happiness. It felt good to be close to someone like this and to let it happen, without fear, without awkwardness or embarrassment. To just feel it and let it happen. He pulled away and smiled at me. I didn't want to rip his clothes off or anything, but the kiss made me feel good. It made me feel better, at peace and happy, in a way I hadn't. Except when Luc had held me.

~ ☾ ~

16 Afterglow

The party sealed the deal. Mo and I stayed up all night until the sun started to sprout up over the horizon. We talked about everything. I learned about his dad, how he had left years ago, but now comes around every year or so, or at least what started out as every year or so, to visit. Mo said the older he got, the longer the time between visits became. He told me his mom had gotten worse and worse since his father left, going deeper and deeper into herself.

I told him about the accident, about how I missed my friends, but also my mom and my dog… all of it. It felt as though a weight had been lifted, and our conversation came naturally. I really liked this guy, and he seemed really into me, too.

I didn't remember my curfew since I never had one with my mom, because at her place it didn't really make a difference. It wasn't that she didn't care. She just trusted me, and believed I would make good choices, would be okay and wouldn't do something stupid. That worked out fine until the night of the accident I guess.

A few people trickled past, heading home. The sun started to rise, and I realized I had parents to check in with.

"God! I've got to go!" I jumped up. "Ack! You should too!"

"Why? I live here."

"Don't vampires turn to ash when the sun rises?" I teased.

"Nah, they just sparkle." He grinned.

~ ☾ ~

The group of juniors from the theater walked passed us and stopped.

"Tim, don't." Cassie grabbed Tim's Jedi robe.

"It's all right," he told her, pulling away. Then he looked right at me. "You shouldn't be here."

I took a few steps back. "I'm sorry?"

"You shouldn't be here... not with them." He waved his arm casually toward Mo. Cassie looked at me apologetically. My drunk radar didn't go off. They seemed completely sober and genuine. Hillary stood back smugly, arms folded across her chest. I looked to Mo who just smirked at them.

"Really, Timmy? That's all you've got?"

"Sometimes, that's all it takes," Tim answered. "We're not like you."

"Oh, believe me, I'm well aware."

"Come on, Tim. This isn't a good idea." Cassie tried to pull him away.

"Why not?" Then super pretty Hillary, in her sexy witch costume, with her platinum blonde, long layered hair and thick bangs side swiped across her brows spoke up. I think she was a cheerleader or Homecoming Queen or some crazy popular royalty. "They should be ashamed of themselves."

Cassie sighed. "Let's just go. Come on Hillary. Tim." They weren't moving. "Fine." She walked away on her own.

"I don't understand," I said. "We're not doing anything wrong."

"It's very simple. You. Shouldn't. Be. Here." Tim emphasized each word slowly, as if I were a moron.

"You're here," I protested, pretty sick of the weird high school politics between the juniors and the seniors and their cryptic almost gang like threats. But if Tim with his preppy spiked hair and salon-highlighted tips led a gang, I'd eat my good witch crown.

~ ☾ ~

Just then, Luc, Sean and Violet came out the front door. I hadn't seen Violet all evening, just heard her shrieking, and had to stifle a laugh. She was wearing the same sexy witch costume as Hillary. *Definitely* glad I didn't buy that one.

"Is there a problem?" Luc asked. I tried not to swoon, having just spent the night with his best friend and thinking I'd made my decision.

"No, no problem for us." Tim held up his arms as though Luc had a real gun and backed away toward Cassie. "For her? That's another story." He stuck a thumb in my direction. He turned and Hillary followed, flipping her hair as she went.

"Let me take care of him." Sean, dressed as a pirate, was chomping at the bit to fight again, the side of his mouth bruised from earlier. Luc just held up a hand, almost a military style signal, and Sean held back.

I stood there, confused as hell. "What the…"

"Are you okay?" Luc asked approaching me.

"You keep asking me that."

"Don't pay attention to them." Mo interrupted.

"They're just jealous," Violet added.

"Of what?"

The seniors stood and watched as the juniors got in Tim's white Kia Soul and sped past, dangerously close. No one answered me or offered further explanation. Luc looked at me like he wanted to say something, then at Mo, but stayed silent. He turned and left. Sean followed and Violet jumped up on Luc's back for a piggyback ride. He obliged.

"Are you going to be all right? Are you going to get in trouble?" Mo asked deftly changing the subject. The sun came up over the horizon as the darkness around Mo's house faded.

"Hmmm, let's see… sunrise? Probably. Sorry you missed your party, hanging out on the curb with me all night."

~ ☾ ~

Speak of the Devil

"I'm not." He took my chin with his fingers and lifted my face up to his making me stop for a second. Then he leaned in and kissed me. So much warmth.

I pulled back and smiled. "I should go."

"If you're already five hours late, what's a few more minutes going to do?"

"Ha, well see, *you* aren't the one who has to find out!"

"Call me later!"

"I don't call boys." I grinned as I headed to my car.

"Good, cuz I'm not a boy! Heck, I'm not even human!" He spread his cape out like bat wings.

Eye roll. I got into my car and before I slammed the door I heard him say, "I'll call you later." I figured maybe I was a natural at this dating thing after all. But as I pulled away I couldn't help wondering what Luc and Violet had been up to all night.

~ ☾ ~

17 Happiness Squashed

Driving home my mind raced and I couldn't wipe the grin off my face. I replayed everything over and over in my head. I loved the feeling of newfound love or like or whatever. I almost felt happy again, having someone attracted and interested in me and having fun with that person, feeling nervous when he was around, but no butterflies yet. Those suckers weren't things you could just call up on demand. Butterflies were very special and rare. I'd only felt them a few times before. With Luc and before with...

Damn it! I tried to turn my brain off at this point. *Damn it, damn it, damn it!* Always... I always went there. In all actuality even with the evening Mo and I just had, we had already surpassed the stage I had been with Mike. Mike and I, in all seriousness, had flirted around each other at school, in math, by the lockers, and had gone to one, short school dance where I was so incredibly shy I spent most of the night hiding with Julie because I hadn't known what to do. We'd shared a few dances together and one kiss on the cheek good-bye.

And then I lost it, thinking about that, not that the dance with Mike had meant much at the time, but at the thought that I had been his first date and last. As I drove home the tears came, slowly at first, and once again the floodgates burst. Cries turned to sobs and became so great I had to pull the car over since I couldn't see anymore. Luckily I had taken the back way home, instead of the main highway. I pulled off the old highway that ran along the river, and wept.

~ ☾ ~

Speak of the Devil

The dance hadn't seemed like anything at the time, because we all assumed there would be more, but for him, there wouldn't be. So Mike had died, having one ridiculously uncomfortable first date and a kiss on the cheek as being the height of romance of his life. It made me feel incredibly sad and guilty and selfish. Mike would never go to another dance, fall seriously in love, go to prom, make love or even have sex. My lousy, embarrassing kiss on the cheek was it for him. God, I hated myself.

I stared out over the Missouri River, a big time river, not like little Black Water River which was pretty much a glorified creek. Unfortunately, the Black Water had been big enough to drown my two closest friends in.

Buzz kill, huh? I had to get away from this water. I kept remembering going under, the water rushing in, and the inability to breathe in the darkness. I started to hyperventilate. *Drive, Lily. Get out of here. Get home.* Crap, I'd forgotten all about having to deal with Dad and Cheryl.

When I got home, I opened the door and heard the footsteps closing in immediately. "Where the hell have you—" my dad started.

I looked up, horrified. *Oh right, parents, curfews, rules and stuff.* This was hardly fair having come from mom's to here with no sort of orientation or guidebook to overprotective parents. "Dad I'm so sorry. I shouldn't have come in so late."

"Honey, are you ok?" Cheryl came up from behind dad to ask. I must have looked a complete disaster, up all night and crying for the last half hour; makeup smeared, eyes puffy and red, costume askew. For a split second I wondered if I should play it to my advantage, but I decided to go with truth.

"Yeah, I'm fine. This? Nothing happened, I just got sad on the way home. I'm fine."

~ ☾ ~

She came and put her arm around me while Dad stood in the back with the tough look on his face but confusion in his eyes. "You should have called," he blurted.

"I know. I lost track of time. I'm sorry."

"Are you hungry?" she asked.

I hadn't been hungry in a while. "No, I think I'll just go lie down for a while." I noticed Owen and Sophie peering around the top of the stairs to listen. I trudged up to my room, and my brother and sister scrambled out of the way.

"Nicely played," Owen admired.

"There was no play. There could have been, but there wasn't."

Since I'd died earlier this year, my parents appreciated my existence more than I did. I think that gave me more leeway than I would have had.

As I closed my bedroom door I heard raised voices from downstairs. I felt for them. They had no idea how to deal with me, and I had no idea how to deal with anything, really. I needed sleep or unconsciousness, at least. Maybe I was bipolar. I went from happy to depressed so fast I couldn't keep it all straight. I just needed to forget what happened somehow. Maybe I should start drinking… a strange thing for me to come up with, but I understood now why people need that kind of escape.

I peeled the good witch costume off layer by layer, losing the wand, the crown, the wings, the shoes, the eyelashes, the poufy dress, until I was just me again, in my bra and panties.

I put on a long Batgirl t-shirt, found some ear buds, lay down and listened to my mp3 player to tune out. My newspaper kit lay on my desk beside the bed, and I paused. Usually we used digital, computer layouts and worked online, but this week we were to work on them

~ ☾ ~

manually, so basically she'd given us a scrapbooking type kit. In it were a small paper cutter, some plastic frames and stencils, an Exacto knife and some razor blade refills. It had never occurred to me before, but this morning, I picked up one of the blades and held it, staring at the thin edge for a long, long time.

~ ☾ ~

18 The Pieces

    I don't know how long I stared at the blade. Since the accident, my life seemed to have been smashed to bits. I tried at first to put it all back together, but every time I got close, I would stumble and drop it all. It would smash again into a thousand pieces. I'd slipped into the "don't care" mode and had quit trying, but then, Mo and Luc and even Belle had tried to help me put it back together again.
    I felt like Humpty Dumpty. Maybe I couldn't be put back together again. Maybe I'd just be in pieces for the rest of my life. I knew that happened to people. I mean look at Mo's weird mom. She had been an art lover once, for God's sake. To look at her now, you'd never know she'd loved anything. She stared out the window, an empty shell. And I was a dead girl. Maybe that was my future.
    If God existed why did he make us so fragile?
    I didn't know what to do. I didn't want to be sad. I didn't want to be happy. I really didn't want to be anything. I got it. I got why the others back home had started drinking more and then turned to drugs. They didn't want anything either. I ran the edge of my thumb along the edge of the blade, not quite hard enough to cut. Then I put the blade in my billfold behind my driver's license. I didn't want to use it today, but maybe later I'd have the courage to, or would it be the cowardice to? I didn't care. I just knew if I wanted it, it would be there.
    Then I slept.

~ ☾ ~

Speak of the Devil

And slept.

And slept.

Throughout the hours I lay there, I awakened from time to time and noticed the position of the sun as it slid across the sky to darkness, and there I lay, still mostly sleeping. A few times Owen or Cheryl had come to the door knocking quietly to see if I wanted or needed anything. I'd say no, and then sleep some more.

The first time my cell phone rang, I put it on silent, but throughout the day, it vibrated. I glanced at the display. Mo. I rolled over and went back to sleep.

Did they have mental hospitals where people just slept their lives away? Maybe I should look into that, I thought. I could think of worse ways to spend your life.

I thought the sleep would help with the healing, pass the time, and put some distance between me and the almighty accident. Or at least I'd get some rest. But each time my phone woke me up, I still felt exhausted, tense, unhinged.

Saturday had come and gone, and then the house got quiet after darkness fell. I realized everyone had gone to bed. At least maybe I'd be undisturbed for a stretch anyway.

Then the texts started coming from Mo. "Are you ok?", "Did you get in trouble?", "Is everything all right?", "I've been thinking about you all day. I can't get you out of my mind." Then an email. "I wrote a song for you since your name keeps running through my head. Your hair, your eyes, your mouth. I want you to hear it. When can you come over again or are you grounded for life?"

I didn't even know if I was grounded or not. Good question.

The texts got more frequent. "Seriously, are you ok?" until the last one. "I'm coming over."

Crap, I'd have to get up now and deal with this. "No!" I replied quickly, before he drove over.

~ ☾ ~

"I was worried. You haven't answered all day."

"Grounded. Going to bed. Talk to you tomorrow," I texted back.

"K, if you're sure."

"Yup sure."

I lay back down and tried to figure out how to pick up the pieces this time or if I should just stop trying.

~ ☾ ~

19 Through the Motions

    Sunday came and went. Lucky for me, my dad didn't ground me, though I'd told Mo he had. I almost wished I were. The lie gave me the excuse to stay home and be alone.
    "You shouldn't stay home in bed all the time," Owen said, peeking into my room.
    "Go away," I rolled over.
    He did, which made me feel crummy, but I didn't need advice from a middle schooler. Seriously.
    Mo texted constantly all weekend, and I lied again saying my dad had taken my phone. "Dad just wanted me to tell you, so my phone would quit buzzing around his desk."
    "K," Mo answered. You can't read much into a "K" response. Did he buy it? Did I care?
    Monday, I would have stayed in bed all day and played sick, but Cheryl worked at home, so I would have to deal with her checking on me. I figured I might as well go through the motions and go to school even though Mo would be all over me all day.
    Don't care mode was similar to walking dead girl mode. I just moved myself from place to place like a zombie following my schedule. I must have looked like hell. I couldn't remember if I'd put makeup on or not. Probably not. Car. School.
    The October air hit me as I got out of my car, cold and crisp. It wrapped its cold, skeletal fingers around me. October was cold and dead like me.
    Mo accosted me as soon as I entered the doors by the theater.

~ ☾ ~

"So they let you out on good behavior to go to school?" he smiled.

I laughed weakly.

"Is it that bad?" he continued.

"What?"

"The trouble you're in. You look, forgive me for saying this, awful. Are you all right? I mean, really?"

Too many questions for me already. I wasn't even to my locker yet. "Yeah, it'll be fine. I'm just tired and cold today." Not sure why I added that, but I'd just worn a short sleeved Spiderman t-shirt that day, not thinking or caring to bring a coat.

"Oh." Again, I couldn't read anything into it, but I didn't care anyway. I shuffled like a zombie to my locker and repeated in my head over and over my schedule for the day; LA 3, Algebra II, Journalism, off block.

He trailed along. "Lily…" Then he just stopped. He probably didn't know what to say, and I didn't blame him. I closed him out, like I closed everyone out.

"I'm fine. Really, but I should get to class. I'll talk to you after, okay? I promise."

Saying more than two words to him helped. He exhaled sharply, relieved. "Okay." And he wandered off.

Zombies don't move very quickly, so I was late for language arts class. "Miss Tyler, a word," Mr. Herb Potter said as I staggered in. Maybe he thought I was drunk.

He pulled me out into the empty hall and closed the door. "Do you want to explain why you're late and why you are in this state?" My teacher looked me up and down.

How could I explain I was a zombie? "Overslept and ran late today. Sorry about that."

"Why?"

Hmmm, I didn't know where to start. Every explanation I had seemed to begin at my death, at the

~ ☾ ~

accident because everything that had happened since seemed to be a result of it especially this funk I was in. "I worked all weekend and stayed up late last night." The lies were beginning to flow fairly easily now. Not only did I now get why my peers turned to alcohol and drugs, I also got why they lied. It was so much easier than the truth.

"Miss Tyler, how old are you?"

"Seventeen." Mr. Potter was one of my favorite teachers, but sometimes I just really didn't know what the hell he was talking about or where he was going with something.

"When is your birthday?"

I wanted to crack a joke about whether he was getting me a present, but he glared at me, stone serious, so I thought better of it. Besides, zombies don't tell jokes.

"April fourteenth."

"That's six months away. Until the day when you turn eighteen, your job is that of a student. If you are unable to work and still perform all duties and tasks of a high school student, you should stop working or learn to prioritize," he said sternly. Then he softened a bit. "You'll have time to work the rest of your life. Now is the time to learn and try to enjoy high school."

Oooohoooo, enjoy high school. It was a fantabulous joyride so far, I thought. "Okay." I didn't really know what to say, especially since I'd just totally lied about working. "Thanks Mr. Potter."

He directed me back into class. As I sat down and took my books out of my backpack, Mo and Luc arrived at the door. I sat in the front row closest to the door, so they peeked cautiously at me, and then to Herb who had turned to the board to jot some notes while discussing *Hamlet*. Mo quickly hurried in and put a blanket around my shoulders. "I had this in my car," he whispered before dashing away.

~ ☾ ~

Potter turned around, having detected some disturbance in the force, but didn't see Mo. My eyes widened and my heart stopped for fear of getting in trouble for the second time in sixty seconds. Potter acknowledged me with a weird look, seeing me seated there wrapped in a not so subtle yellow blanket. He furrowed his brows and went on with his lecture.

"God she's a waste," someone whispered behind me.

"Freakin' nut job," another student added to it.

I felt my face flush. Lily Tyler, formerly a straight-A student, non-drinking, non-smoking, honest, virginal, fun-loving Mid-Western girl from the country, had turned into an emotionally out of control, apathetic, lying catastrophe who may or may not pass the eleventh grade. I would have asked myself how it had come this, but I knew. The former version of me had died. Literally and figuratively.

I turned to see who had said the words, out of curiosity, not out of vengeance or anger or anything. Just shock. And there they were, two of the drama juniors again. Spiky haired Tim and Barbie Hillary. What was their deal? I gave them a look reflecting that sentiment. I raised my eyebrows and my hands, non-verbally asking them for more. "Is there something you'd like to say to me?" I added when they didn't respond.

Tim looked down, his face reddening, clearly not having meant to be heard, but Hillary smirked at me.

"What is your problem?" I asked more loudly than I'd intended.

"Miss Tyler, do I need to take you into the hall once again?"

I realized I should go back to going through the motions before I got too sidetracked.

~ ☾ ~

20 I Give

I survived the next class, but then they caught me.
"Hey! Lily!" Mo ran up to me. "Come with us."
"I'm not done for the day."
"Yes, but as soon as you get home you're back in isolation. Come with us." Mo bounced on the balls of his feet.
I gave him a confused look. "Huh?" I forgot which lies I'd told to whom.
"If you can't hang out with us after school, then we have to use our time wisely," he said.
"Oh." I didn't know what he was getting at, but didn't want to say "huh" again.
"Just come with us!" Behind Mo, stood Luc. He grinned at me, so I had to
look at the others or become paralyzed. Sean and Belle were there, too.
I wasn't the arguing, confrontation type, and if I were truly in don't-care-zombie just going-through-the-motions mode, what did it matter? After all, I wasn't even truly grounded... yet.
"What the hell." I shrugged. Mo took me by one arm, and Sean moved in and grabbed me by the other. They hurried to the back doors by the theater. "Wait, what? Where are we going?" I noticed Luc seemed to be keeping a respectful distance.
"We're kidnapping you," Mo said.
Yeah, I was less sure about this. They led me out to Sean's van, opened the side door, and
in Belle and I went. Mo sat in the back with us and

~ ☾ ~

Luc took shotgun. Sean sped off.

"Are you all done for the day?" I asked. Sean laughed and Luc smirked.

"Not exactly." Belle smiled her bright smile.

Skipping school. This was new. Sure, why not? Being a goody-goody hadn't gotten me

anywhere. It had gotten me killed is all. Sean pulled out of the parking lot and we were off. Sean drove an old delivery van with no seats in the back, so the three of us were just sitting on the floor. Before we even made it to the highway, Belle opened a cooler in the back.

"Don't mind if I do." She took a beer out and twisted the top. Mo just shook his head. I must not have been in truly don't care mode because my mind started racing, counting the number of laws we were breaking: truancy, underage drinking, and an open container in a moving vehicle. I tried not to hyperventilate.

Sean turned up the stereo, pumping the Silversun Pickups "The Royal We" through the van, *"How many times do you want to die?"*

Damn, hyperventilation commencing. Did Belle not get it? Did any of them? What the hell? What was wrong with them? Didn't they realize I'd already died? *In a car crash?*

"I can't do this. I can't—" Panic attack in 5…4…3…2…

"Here." Belle handed me a beer. "Just drink."

After all that had happened, after all the ways I'd tried to cope and had failed miserably, and after all I'd left back home for… maybe she had a point. I'd tried to pretend the accident had never happened by running away. I'd cried constantly. I'd shouted at and cursed and denied God. I'd pushed my family away. I'd felt guilt for being alive. I'd gone numb. I even carried a razor blade around in my purse. I lied. I'd become a zombie. Depression still clung to me like cigarette smoke stuck to you after leaving a party. They were still dead.

~ ☾ ~

Speak of the Devil

Maybe the kids back home had it figured out from the beginning. Maybe they'd gotten drunk, taken some drugs and gotten over it. Maybe they were all laughing and guilt free for being alive. Maybe Belle had a point. But these friends of Mo's had seemed so different.

She held the bottle toward me and a little voice, like the devil on my shoulder seemed to whisper in my ear, echoing her words: "Just drink."

I took the bottle. Alice drank and turned really, really small. Maybe if I drank enough I'd disappear. Wonderland had to be better than high school.

"Really?" Luc snapped suddenly. When I glanced his way, I saw he directed this question at Mo, not Belle, which seemed strange since she was offering me the drink. "This is your solution?"

Mo's eyes lit up as he sat eagerly watching me to see if I'd drink or not. I moved the bottle slightly as if to drink.

"Mo!" Luc shouted.

"What?" Mo answered, impatiently.

"This is it? This is how you help her? You think this is going to do the trick?"

Mo glared at Luc, but didn't have a response. Sean drove, head bobbing as he danced to the music, and Belle drank.

Sometimes you've gotta say, what the hell? So I drank.

"It's not like it's the end of the world," Mo said. Luc turned around in the passenger seat, not saying anything. He just shook his head.

I didn't like the gross taste of beer, but I knew I wasn't drinking it for the taste. I could either suffer consciously or be at peace, albeit temporarily, unconsciously. Mo reached around me for the cooler, and started drinking himself.

We drove for a while. I didn't know where since I sat on the floor in the back. I think I'd had three beers and

~ ☾ ~

could already feel it. Belle, Mo and I were extremely happy at this point.

"Why do I always have to drive?" Sean grumbled from the front.

"This is unbelievable," Luc complained to himself. "This isn't going to work."

"It will be fun whether it works or not." Mo put his arm around me and moved in for a quick kiss. I let him, but really just wanted some space. I had a lot to process. *Why do they always talk about me like I'm not there? Or not even human?* I wondered.

"Screw this. Stop the van," Luc ordered.

"No," Sean answered.

"Stop the van, now!"

"No!"

"I told you to stop the damn van!"

"And I said, 'no'." Sean accelerated.

Things were getting awkward. I finished my beer and not being a big drinker, I already felt no pain, but even half buzzed I could still detect the tension.

Luc rolled down his window. "Fine," he said. Then he climbed out.

I wondered how much I'd had to drink because surely I was hallucinating or imagining things. But it was pretty clear. Luc reached up, pulled himself to a sitting position in the window, and climbed out and up to the top of the van.

Sean started laughing. "Crazy prick."

Mo nearly spit out his beer laughing so hard. Belle didn't seem to notice it at all, but this definitely sobered me up.

"What the hell?" I leapt up to the shotgun seat and searched frantically out all of the windows.

"It's fine," Sean, the only sober one left in the vehicle, said. "Chill out."

"Fine? Fine? How is this fine?" I checked the

~ ☾ ~

speedometer. Sean was driving 75 mph. "You'll kill him! Jesus!" Cue the panic attack. Drinking, driving, friend on top of van as it speeds down the highway. More laws being broken. I couldn't breathe.

No one in the van reacted to this at all, so I did the unthinkable. I climbed out of the window, too.

Immediately the tires screeched to a stop, and I held on for dear life.

"What the hell are you doing?" Sean roared as he tried to maneuver safely to a stop.

I looked up over the top of the van from my sitting position in the window, holding on to the roof. Luc wasn't there.

"What the hell!" I shouted as the van finally stopped. "He's gone! He must have fallen off!"

"Lily, get in the van."

"Go back! Turn around and find him!" I screamed hysterically, looking around the side of the van. "Call 911!"

"Lily, get in the van." I felt a hand on my knee and a wave of warmth rushed through me. I knew that touch. I knew that voice. I climbed back in to see for myself.

"Luc?"

"Come on." He sat calmly in the back, reaching out to me to come to him.

As was becoming a bit of a habit, I fell into his embrace, a confused, shuddering, crying disaster.

~ ☾ ~

21 WTF?

Luc was in the van.

"But how... where did...what?" I stammered, wiping away the tears with the back of my hand.

He and Mo just gave each other sideways glances.

"What do you mean?" Sean asked.

I looked at each of them, in the eyes. They stared back blankly.

"What do I mean? Luc climbed out of the van, onto the top of the van, and disappeared only to reappear inside the van."

"How is that possible?" Mo asked.

"Exactly!"

They just looked at me like I was insane.

"Look, guys, I'm not a moron, and I'm not entirely drunk, and although my drinking experience has, granted, been limited up until now, I did get an A in Health and am aware that drinking alcohol doesn't cause you to hallucinate."

"Honey," Belle said putting her arm around me. "Nothing happened." She sounded completely sober.

I shoved her arm off. "Bull. That is bull and you know it!"

They just sat there staring except for Luc whose face was downcast, fascinated with his All-Stars. I knew there was something they weren't telling me and noticed Luc hadn't said anything else, so I directed the next question at him.

"How did you do it?"

His sat up straight, pulling back and shook his head,

~ ☾ ~

Speak of the Devil

taken aback that I'd asked him directly. But he paused, "Do… what?" I could read it, the regret in his eyes though, and he immediately broke eye contact. He didn't like lying to me, but for some reason he was.

There had been something strange with this group from day one, and I'd put it down to… I don't know what. Me not understanding what they were talking about maybe? Me not hearing exactly what they'd said? The pieces were falling into place now, but I couldn't make out the big picture.

These weren't typical high school seniors. Their performance at the Renaissance Festival had been my first surprise, smooth, uninhibited, not your typical high school students standing on a stage in front of an audience. Then the way I'd overheard them talking, what had seemed like they were talking about *it* being theirs and them finding *it*, but in reflection, seemed to be *me*. The way Luc and Mo fought over me like dogs with a bone. Mo's mom. Luc directing questions to Mo about how he's going to save me, like I'm some sort of mission or project. Then this… I didn't know what it all meant, but I knew it meant something.

"Take me back." I buckled my seat belt and faced the front.

"What? Why?" Mo started in.

"Take me. The hell. Back."

"Do it," Luc ordered.

Sean obeyed him this time, and they drove me to school, no one saying a word the entire way. When we arrived, they dropped me off at my car at the otherwise empty parking lot. We'd skipped the whole day. I grabbed my things and climbed out.

"Lily, wait," Luc said, but I slammed the door as a reply and unlocked my car.

The side van door opened and Mo came out. "Lily, let me explain."

~ ☾ ~

I turned and waited, but he just stood there, and looked helplessly back to Luc and Belle who were watching from the van.

"Waiting." I crossed my arms and tapped my index finger impatiently.

He just sort of shrugged. I threw my books and bag in the back seat of my car.

"I've spilled my guts to you guys but there's something you clearly aren't letting me in on! Are you trying to make me crazy? Crazier rather? I don't need this crap! I've got my own issues to deal with, which you all know about! So tell me what the hell is going on."

"Lily."

"I'm aware of my name. You don't have to keep saying it."

"Are you okay to drive?" he asked weakly.

"Oh, good one, knowing my history and about my friends. That's a low blow."

Sean piped up from the driver's seat. "Alcohol clearly doesn't agree with her. She's a mean drunk."

"Go to hell," I said. This, for some reason, brought out a burst of laughter from Sean. I shook my head and got in my car. "Freak shows," I mumbled and slammed the door. Mo stood there looking hopeless while I sped off squealing my tires.

I glanced back in the rear view as I waited to pull out of the parking lot. Sean parked the van and the four of them headed inside. Rehearsal I imagined. I drove down the road for a few minutes then thought, *I'm not grounded. I don't have to be home.* I really wanted to see what these people were up to, so I turned around and parked out front in the teachers' parking lot. I took my phone, put it on silent, and headed down to where I knew they'd all be — the theater.

~ ☾ ~

22 You Wouldn't Believe Me if I Told You

    I made my way to the theater, listening from outside the front doors. I could hear voices, but nothing specific. I had to get closer if I wanted to hear anything, so I slipped down the side hall where I'd heard them before, outside the dressing rooms. They were quiet, so I slipped in.
    "Well, it was stupid," Luc said. "You could have lost her. You may have."
    Perfect. They were talking about me, most likely. I wanted to see them, so I could tell who he spoke to. I knew it was probably Mo, but I wanted to get a good look. I hadn't spent much time in the dressing rooms, so I snooped to see where the best spying vantage point would be. A door led out to the side hallway, and some steps headed up to another door to the stage. The rest of the room housed a makeup table with a large, ornate mirror. A rack of costumes lined one wall, and a large cabinet full of props sat against the opposite wall. Handbags, hats, wigs, canes and were stashed haphazardly around the room, providing lots of places to hide if any of them happened to come down, but I didn't want to get caught hiding in there.
    Then I noticed it, a ladder going up to a trapdoor in the ceiling mounted along the wall behind the costume racks. *Go big or go home*, I thought, quietly crawling under the costumes and going up the ladder to see where it led.

~ ☾ ~

"You were the one who climbed out of the freakin' van!" I heard Mo say. *I knew it! I* knew *I wasn't drunk or crazy!* I thought, pushing the door in the ceiling over as quietly as I could.

Pulling myself up, all I could see at first was darkness. My eyes adjusted eventually and the stage lights filtered in. Another ladder led straight up for some distance from the side of the stage, to an intricate crisscross of bars and boards and lights. Way up above rested the catwalk.

I couldn't see them yet but could hear them much better from my new vantage point. The stage curtains blocked my view of them and luckily theirs of me. However, if they came backstage for anything, I'd be seen. I sighed quietly and figured if I wanted to remain hidden, I had to go up.

"I told Sean to stop the van," Luc said from below.

I climbed up about fifty feet. Even though I was farther away, the set up of the stage acoustics allowed me to hear every word as it carried up and out for the audience. I ventured ahead to the catwalk, which would put me directly overhead where I could get a good look.

"So what?" Sean jumped in.

"So what? So I'm in charge here, that's what!"

I hunkered down and just lay at the very edge of the catwalk, so I could see them all perfectly now. Luc stood near the center of the stage and paced back and forth. Mo and Sean sat on the edge of the stage, legs hanging over the side. Belle, Mya and Violet were seated in the front row, not saying anything yet. A few rows back I could see Gregor lying across three of the seats, probably sleeping. I wondered if he had a medical condition. I lay down on my stomach, the best way to be balanced so far above the stage, and pulled myself forward quietly along the catwalk, staying flat so if anyone happened to glance up, they would be hard

~ ☾ ~

Speak of the Devil

pressed to see me. If I'd known I was going stealth that day, I would've worn black.

Sean snorted at Luc, who turned on him, towering over him. Sean cowered like a chastised dog.

"You would do well to remember that. All of you!" Luc faced the others in the audience.

I had to wonder what he meant. "I'm in charge here"? What the hell? Why the hell didn't the drama teacher ever come to the theater, and why did these guys have the run of the theater all day and after school. I pulled myself forward a little more, starting to experience vertigo at the height. The catwalk was filthy, probably not traveled very much. As I pulled myself along the boards, my shirt collected the dust. I accidently brushed a small dust bunny loose, and it lightly floated down to the stage. I held my breath hoping no one would notice. To me it was obvious, but luckily it made its way safely down and none of them reacted.

I wondered what Gregor, Mya and Violet were doing there. They hadn't been involved.

"Look, Luc," Violet started in. "I get that you're upset."

"No. No, I'm not upset. I think it's time you, all of you, sat and listened and remembered what we're doing here."

Violet shut up.

"We know why we're here." Mo sat sulking, eyes toward the floor.

"Do you? Do you really? Because I think we could all use a little freakin' reminder!" Luc turned to the seats. "Gregor! Wake the hell up!" he shouted.

Greg jumped. "I'm up. I'm up!"

"Have you imbeciles considered lately what is happening?" No one answered. "Why do you think so many of us were stationed here? Hmmm?" The girls slunk down in their seats. Belle had acquired a bag of

~ ☾ ~

chips from somewhere and munched loudly, attracting a look from Luc. How she maintained such a gorgeous body the way she ate, I had no idea.

Luc went on. "Angels generally work in a solitary fashion, yet here we have more than a dozen of us. Think about it!" he shouted.

Wait, what? Angels... what could he mean? Was that the name of their theater group or some weird gang? And a dozen? I only saw seven of them.

"Why do you morons think that is?" he asked softly. No one answered. "Sean? Mya?"

"Because something big is going down," Mo offered.

Luc paced the stage, eyeing each of them in turn. "Something big. Something big and something awful. So here we are having parties, using up our earthly parents, drinking, dicking with people... Do you think you're ready for whatever is coming? Do you think the juniors are?"

Mya shook her head no.

He continued. "No, Mya. You're right. We're not."

I had no clue what he meant or what the juniors had to do with it.

"It's not our frigging fault!" Sean shouted.

Walking across the stage to him, Luc answered. "No? It's not our fault? Jesus Christ, forgive my brothers. Whose fault is it, Sean? Let's hear it."

"His."

"His. Sure, His. How the hell do you figure?"

"Sean's right," Violet offered. "He's abandoned us here without guidance or direction."

In a burst of speed I'd never seen any human have, Luc leaped from the stage and in an instant his hand clutched her throat. "No guidance? What the hell do you think I am?"

Her eyes widened and her hands grasped fruitlessly at his.

~ ☾ ~

He released her, walking away disgusted. "I have tried to give you direction for years. I have tried to get you to rein in your humanity, yet all of you act like this is some big damn vacation! How many of you have looked in her eyes?"

Mo and Belle reluctantly raised their hands.

"Exactly. Was it fun and games in there?" They shook their heads. "No, it's not. That girl is this close from…" He trailed off as though he were too emotional to continue on about me.

"She's broken," Belle filled in. My eyes welled up. Everyone around me could see my pain.

"Put the damned chips down, Belle." Luc lunged at her and swatted the bag away. Then he practically flew over two rows to get back to Greg who reclined in his seat. "And wake the hell up!" he roared, slapping Greg's legs from the seats so he'd be in a seated position. "It's obvious to me. How about you? Can't you guys see it? Can you *see* what we're becoming?"

"We're lost, Luc." Mya's voice cracked slightly.

"Whether we are lost or not, it's up to us! Find yourselves!" Luc ran his hands through his hair and shook his head. "If we can't find ourselves, if we can't save our own damned selves, who will? How the hell are we supposed to help her? How the hell are we supposed to help *any* of them?"

No one answered him as he climbed back up on stage and walked to the center where the lights were brightest and seemed to reflect from him. He stared at his feet briefly, raised his head and faced them all, looking like he glowed. "Yes, you are right and we have a sense of loss ourselves. We have no direct contact from Him. We haven't in years, but really, has our purpose changed? Are we really going to sit here and say we don't know what we're supposed to do? Has being human affected your brains so much?" He paced up to Sean. "When you

~ ☾ ~

were initially placed, what was your direction?"

Sean turned from him. Luc took Sean's face in his hands forcing him back to look him in the eyes. "I asked you a question. What was your mission?"

"Same as everyone else's!" Sean jerked his head away.

"Mo? Would you care to answer me? See this is the problem right here. Mo?"

"We were placed to save a soul," Mo answered eyes still downcast.

"Yes, thank you. To save a soul… have you pondered that recently? Any of you? Do you realize what significance that has? He placed a great amount of trust in us to complete our task, yet we're playing crazy teenagers down here. Are you focused? Have you found your soul?"

"We think so," Belle answered.

"No, you haven't. We don't all have the same soul. To each his or her own. We each get one to save, and we can't even agree on that one little element! We have fourteen angels all placed in the same city in the same school, for God's sake, at the same freakin' time! We should all be actively looking and not fighting over the same one! We can't all save her… hell the way we're going, no one will. We'll just drive her to the edge like we have our parents!"

None of this made any sense to me, and frankly it all freaked me out. Maybe this was a play they'd written and were rehearsing, a prank they were playing? I didn't know if I wanted to hear anything else.

"Lily has suffered more than a girl should, and we're arguing and acting like a bunch of idiots. Is she any closer to being saved?" He looked around, and silence answered. "Belle, you looked in her eyes. Where are we with that?"

"She's lost… just like we are."

"We are not lost! We are here and we are angels!" he

~ ☾ ~

roared. Then he seemed to weaken and slumped to the stage, his head in his hands. "We can't be lost." He looked up. "No, we can't be lost. Mo!" he moved manically to Mo and grabbed him. "You've looked in her eyes. What did you see?" he asked, taking his hands off him.

Mo took a deep breath. "Grief. Loss. Hopelessness."

"So you get her drunk and paw her and screw with her."

Mo turned away.

"If we want to help ourselves, we have to help them. Lily's eyes...," he paused, directly below me. "For those who have bothered to look, Lily's eyes are blue. Lily's eyes are full of pain and guilt and confusion. Lily is on the edge of tears at any given moment. When I look at her... " He stopped again, his voice cracking.

"Sean, I want you to look in her eyes the next time you see her. Violet, you too. Lily and those like her are the reason we are here. We aren't lost. She is, and we're exactly where we need to be. Lily was a good, happy person, and you can see that in her eyes too. Impressions of happiness and memories there, trapped in the back of her eyes, and we can read them. It's there. Mo? You've seen them? Belle?" The two of them nodded as they both stared at their feet. "And now, Lily wants to die." He wiped his eyes with the back of his sleeve, and his voice faltered a bit. I think I heard one of the girls sniff.

I realized my eyes were full of tears too. I moved to wipe them away, but my movement caused a tear to fall. I saw it as though it were in slow motion fall toward the stage below and land on Luc's shoulder. He blinked, glanced at it, and looked up.

~ ☾ ~

23 And Another Thing

I pulled back as quickly as I could, hoping to be hidden by the board I lay on. I stopped breathing and held as still as possible. An infinite pause settled upon us.

"What is it?" Mya asked him.

"Sshhh!"

The front doors to the theater suddenly banged open.

"Well, well, well," someone said.

"Not a good time." Luc tried to wave him off.

"What are you talking about, Luc?" Mo asked. "It's the perfect time. These bozos need to hear this as much as we do."

"Hear what, exactly?"

I cautiously leaned a little, so I could see who had entered. Tim and the rest of the juniors came in. "This should be interesting," he said to his friends. I counted seven of them, now making fourteen in total below me.

I hadn't seen all of the juniors together at once. I had at least one class with each of them,

being a junior myself, but I never actually spoke to them. With Tim stood Cassie and the mean Barbie doll, Hillary. Kara flanked them. I'd gotten a quote from Kara at Ren Fest. Dillon, a short, blond guy with braces and the last two I just had algebra with and never heard them actually speak. Patrick was a tall, skinny guy and Nina wore her curly blonde hair in a bun on the top of her head.

"I said this isn't a good time." Luc stood firm.

~ ☾ ~

Speak of the Devil

"Whatever, as though I care," Tim went on. "I didn't exactly come here to listen. I came here to talk."

"Go on then."

"It's clear your 'team' is losing it, so we've come to report—"

"Why you little—" Sean lunged off the stage toward Tim in a blur, but his preternatural speed didn't seem to surprise Tim in the least, who leapt up over him and onto the stage, calmly turning back to Luc.

"As I was saying before I was so rudely interrupted, it's clear some if not all of you are falling."

Sean roared and started after him again, but Greg actually sprang up and held him back,

saying something in his ear to calm him.

"Um — yeah, wrath much?" Tim asked, looking pointedly at Luc.

"Get on with it," Luc ordered.

Tim turned to the seniors and counted off gesturing to the offenders as he read them. "Let's see, sloth." He pointed at Greg. "Gluttony," he said waving to Belle. "Envy," to Violet. "Greed?" He teetered his hand back and forth as if he weren't exactly sure about Mya.

Luc cut him off. "Not on my watch!"

"Pride." Tim smiled too sweetly at Luc. "You see, I'm pretty sure — no, I'm certain of it — falling is a violation."

Violet jumped up. "Who would you go to report us anyway? Have you heard from Him?"

Tim laughed.

"Unfortunately, no, but He isn't the only one who can remove angels from their assignments." This seemed to quiet the others. "I see you know that."

"Been reading your *Angels for Dummies* book again, Timmy?" Mo taunted him.

"We can report you to the archangels." Hillary glared at Mo.

~ ☾ ~

"There's no proof." Luc spoke so softly the only way I heard him was because of the stage acoustics. Belle pushed the bag of chips that had been knocked to the floor in front of her under her seat with her foot.

"As if they'd need proof. Just look at the lot of you. Embarrassing really," Tim told them.

"Your 'team' isn't spotless. Hillary alone probably has half the sins clawing at her already," Mo shouted.

"Screw you!" she shouted up at him, realizing her error, too late.

"Oooohhhhoooooo! You kiss the virgin mother with that mouth?" Mo laughed at his own joke.

"Cast the first stone," Violet taunted her. "I dare you!"

"Look," Luc tried to regain control, "we are all under a great deal of stress and some of our defenses may be weakening…"

"All of them," Tim interrupted.

Ignoring the remark, Luc went on, "…but what all of us need here is to work together. Do you have your souls identified yet?"

The juniors looked from one to the other.

"Do you have a plan of action?"

"Do you?" Hillary threw back.

"No. No we don't, and that's exactly why we're here. We're trying to remember our purpose. We were placed a year before you, so imagine what we're going through."

Hillary stepped forward to say something again, but Tim held a hand up to stop her. "Let him finish."

"We should be training, strategizing, hunting, praying until we know what exactly we're

here for and who we are here to save."

"He's right," Kara agreed.

"Why on earth would we work with you?" Tim asked.

"We are all trying to do the same thing. We work for the same boss."

Tim scoffed.

~ ☾ ~

"Unless, you've fallen?" Luc walked right up to Tim and looked him in the eye. "Pride comes before the fall."

"Don't be ridiculous."

"The reason you see it so easily in me? Because you feel it coming, don't you?"

Shifting uneasily, Tim looked around at his followers.

"He's right, Tim," Cassie answered this time. "We can all feel some form of the sins coming, Luc."

"We're scared," Kara added.

I could see it from high up on the catwalk, their sincerity. They were all scared and they wanted Luc to save them.

My heart pounded and beads of sweat formed on my forehead. Heat collected up at my dizzying height, and I was beginning to feel woozy. *Have I eaten today? Three beers and no food, not good!* I thought I might pass out and doing so up here would be a terrible idea. I figured now was as good a time as any to get down and go before they caught me spying or I fell to my second death.

~ ☾ ~

24 Spinning

    I escaped the theater undetected, I hoped, and hurried out the front to my car that I parked what seemed like an eternity ago. Dizziness — from the information or the alcohol — shifted the ground beneath my feet.

    How I made it home safely, I'm not sure. The roads had been nothing but green, grey, and brown blurs hypnotizing me as they whipped past. I ran inside long enough to blow past Owen and throw my books on my bed, but I kept my tablet. I made sure I'd been seen, or at least heard, by my family but left just as quickly, Owen shouting something at me as I left. It didn't register.

    I raced, running and stumbling and running again, to the gravel road behind the subdivision where the horses would come up to the fence while I cried over my friends. Tears didn't come this time, but even more so than usual, emotions battered me. My usual grief and denial warred with confusion and anger. I just wanted to smash something. *What the hell was happening around me?*

    It neared dinnertime. The breeze swelled up, giving a hint of a cold winter to come, and the wind blew fallen leaves around until they stuck to the ground, wet from a recent rain. The dry air cooled even more, the closer to nightfall it got.

    Hungry, cold, and confused, I took a deep breath, leaned on a tree by the road, facing the horse field and turned on my tablet.

    Okay, Lily. Process, I thought. Breathe and sort it out.

~ ☾ ~

Angels. I typed. Falling, sins, fourteen, mission, catastrophe, Luc, Tim, silence...

I stopped. None of it made sense. Or did it? Maybe it made perfect sense if I opened myself to the possibility.

Something had been strange about this group from the beginning. What else could it be? Luc and Mo and the others were angels.

"How is it possible?" I asked aloud.

"You still don't know? Even after the accident? Even after you died and saw what you saw?" A voice said from the dusk.

A few seconds ticked by, but I eventually recognized it. I fought to keep hysteria out of my voice. "Mike?"

"How is it you still can't see?" he asked.

I turned toward the sound of his voice. His image wavered, translucent before me. He stood with the sunset behind him, and strange colorful lights radiated around him.

After five months of living without him or Julie, after five months of tears and emptiness, after five months of questioning God, religion, and the meaning of life, here he was. Mike, right there in front of me. My breath caught in my chest and I was afraid to move, afraid to speak or do anything that might cause the vision to fade away and leave me alone and lost again. But I couldn't just stand there dumbfounded. Mike was right here with me. I wanted to jump into his arms and hug him, hold him forever, but feared the image would ripple away into nothing if I did, so I proceeded with caution.

"Mike! How can this..." I started but too many questions swirled in my head.

"It just can."

"How? Why are you here?"

"If you had walked into math not believing in the existence of geometry and asked Mr. Cline how can math be? The answer would be the same."

~ ☾ ~

"It just can?"
He smiled.
"It's not fair. Life without you and Julie…".
"I know." He smiled.
"I miss you. Both of you so much!" The tears immediately stung my eyes.
"I miss you, too."
There were too many questions in my head; I couldn't get them out. I stood there dumbstruck.
"It's okay. It's hard, but don't let our death change you. You know."
"I know what?" I asked.
He reached out toward me, and I raised my hand to him, but the sun dipped below the horizon, gone from behind him, and he dissolved with it. I was left alone with the bizarre black and blue bruised twilight sky. "You've seen," his voice echoed from nowhere and faded away.
"Lily," I heard on the wind as I stood, my arm still outstretched toward the darkened horizon.
"Lily!" It came louder and snapped me back to reality. I must have fallen asleep or fallen unconscious, because none of it could have happened. It could not be real. But a pang of new grief gripped my insides. Like I'd just lost him all over again.
I glanced down the road to see Mo and Luc running toward me. "Lily! How did you—?" Mo shouted.
"Lily!" They kept shouting my name as I stood there in shock, watching them run up.
"Who was that?" Luc grabbed my arms and stared in my eyes.
I felt drunk still and dizzy, and nearly giggled. Drunk or slap happy or giddy or crazy. "That was Mike," I answered, matter-of-factly.
Then it hit me; they'd seen him, too. The two of them glanced at each other with stone seriousness.

~ ☾ ~

"Mike?" Mo asked. "Your friend from the car accident."

I nodded.

Releasing me, Luc ran up to the spot where Mike had appeared and searched the area.

"Wait, you saw him, too?" I asked.

Mo looked at me with more gravity than I'd ever seen in him. Typically he acted all happy and bounced around like a big puppy. Now he eyed me as though his life or my life depended on it. He didn't answer me, but reached out and took my arm, like he couldn't let me get away.

I jerked free of his grasp. "Get off me!"

"Lily," he started. "Listen…"

"No. *You* listen. Both of you listen to *me*! The two of you are going to tell me what is going on, once and for all!"

Luc came back shaking his head at Mo. "Nothing." Again, they seemed to forget I was there.

"What?" I asked. "What the hell is going on?"

They looked at one another.

"No, don't look at each other. Look at me, and answer me, now!" I demanded. They avoided my gaze.

I immediately rummaged through my backpack. I felt lost and confused and every answer only brought more questions. I didn't even know if this was real life anymore or a dream. Maybe I was still dead from the crash, and this was purgatory. Maybe they'd slipped something in my drink earlier. I didn't know, but something wasn't right. I found the razor blade in my wallet and held it to my wrist as I spoke.

"One more time. Start talking or I get the answers from your boss, face to face."

~ ☾ ~

25 Revelations

In a blur of super speed to rival the Flash, Luc was on top of me, pushing me down on the ground while gripping my blade holding wrist. "Drop it," he ordered.

I thought about arguing but decided that it was pointless, like everything else, so I released the blade. Quickly Mo scooped it up and pocketed it.

Luc slowly let me go. I glared at him with narrowed eyes and pushed myself up.

"I deserve to—" I started to spit out.

"You're right." His voice was soft and he eyed the ground as he moved to a sitting position, holey knees up like the first time I'd seen him. He ran his hands through his hair before his eyes focused heavenward, and he searched the skies as though he were looking for something… someone.

"What are you saying?" Mo gasped.

"She's right. She deserves to know. She practically does anyway."

"I do?" I asked.

"You were on the catwalk in the theater. You heard all of it," Luc said flatly.

"She *what*?" Mo's voice went up an octave.

"How did you—?" I started again, only to be cut off.

"The tear. I felt the tear. I didn't see you, but I felt you there," Luc explained.

"What are you talking about?" Mo asked.

"It doesn't matter anymore." Luc sighed heavily. "I'm not sure what does."

This I could relate to. "So?" I urged.

~ ☾ ~

Again he sighed, pulling his knees to his chest and casually resting his forearms on them as he looked at me. He bent his head down and ran his hands through his shoulder length hair, before looking up and meeting my gaze.

"Luc, stop, we aren't supposed to..." This time Luc cut Mo off.

"I'm well aware of the rules. If you don't want to be a part of this conversation, feel free to remove yourself from it," Luc reprimanded. Mo glanced around desperately, but stayed put and sat quietly cross-legged by us.

"As you overheard, we are guardians... angels. We're usually assigned at birth to a family in need — a family who will love and care for a child, even sacrifice itself for that child. They get us. Unfortunately, it's a rather sick joke, because eventually, being close to divinity for prolonged periods affects them, negatively," Luc explained.

"Most of them go mad," Mo interjected.

I leaned in.

"So we're placed with a family," Luc continued, "because there is a need for us to be where we're placed. Our task is to save a soul on earth. Usually as babies, we aren't capable of doing so, but often times as young children, we are awakened with the knowledge of who we are and what our purpose is. Sometimes an archangel will appear to us and tell us, sometimes we are just born with the knowledge, and some of the luckier ones speak to God directly."

He said it so casually. "Speak to God?" I blurted out.

He nodded.

"But God—" I started.

"Doesn't exist? I can assure you that at least until very recently, He did."

"Very recently?" I asked.

~ ☾ ~

"God has fallen silent," Mo answered. "No one has spoken to him in over a decade."

"Which is unusual," Luc added. "It's complicated, but while some of us may never have spoken to Him, we, each of the guardians on earth, report to a higher archangel, and they have regular contact with God who oversees… well everything." He gave a short laugh.

"But the archangels…?" I felt almost ridiculous having this conversation. It was so impossible, yet made so much sense at the same time.

"Have heard nothing, zip, nada. Like Mo said, it's been over ten years. Which complicates things further. Without at least secondary contact with Him or being in the presence of home, what you would call Heaven, guardians go through a similar process to what our earthly parents experience. We don't start to go mad, but we—" He broke off to gather his thoughts, and went on. "Let's say you all of a sudden, God forbid, lose both parents or your family or your home, it would affect you in a variety of ways."

"Or lose your friends?" I helped.

"Exactly." Luc met my gaze; his eyes were full of compassion, empathy. "Depression, aimlessness, doubt, temptation… guardians who lose touch with God and who haven't been in the presence of our home—"

"Heaven," I added.

"Right… we start to get lost."

"Some of us fall," Mo said.

"Fall? Like fall? As in become devils?" I asked, my eyes wide.

Neither of the guardians made eye contact, and after a moment, Luc spoke. "It's possible. We start to lose our connection to home, to God, to our own divinity. We become more earthy in our ways, thoughts and behaviors. We become susceptible to sin, like most people do. In extreme cases, if we become completely

Speak of the Devil

lost or fallen, then yes. We could become demons."

"What if that was to happen?"

"We don't speak of it, and quite honestly, I'm not sure what would happen, other than the fact that we wouldn't be allowed to return home."

"Heaven?" I asked, and he nodded. "So you can't go home now, for a quick visit to recharge your divinity?"

Luc didn't say anything at first then exhaled heavily. "Guardians don't return home until our mission is fulfilled and we have saved our soul."

I nodded, letting it all sink in, but slowly the realization of what he said made sense. "You save your soul, and you return home... to Heaven."

Luc nodded, and Mo looked off into the darkness of the horse pasture.

"So if you happen to find your soul tonight and save that person, you don't exist tomorrow?" I asked.

He pursed his lips, nodding. "That's about the way of it."

"Your stay here is temporary." I looked accusingly at Mo, my supposed boyfriend. "That would have been nice to know."

"Look, Lily, we could be here for five more minutes or we could be here for fifty more years," Luc said, trying to explain.

"Don't say that." Mo nearly shuddered. "We've been here eighteen years already."

"It's just like people. They can go at any time," I said, understanding.

"We can't tell people who or what we are," Mo explained.

"Why not? Why not let us all know there's a God when we're suffering, when we've lost faith, when we're tempted?" I nearly shouted at him.

Luc gently put his hand on my knee and warmth radiated through me. "Because that's not what faith is

~ ☾ ~

about. Faith believes without seeing. It would be like giving someone the answers to the test. People don't learn like that, they don't have their own experience. It's not our job."

I nodded and looked down at his hand on me. Everything looked so real, felt so real, but it was as if I were dreaming.

"So how do you know when you've found your soul?"

The guardians both chuckled slightly. "Good question," Mo said.

"I think with the presence of God, it would be clearer. Our directives from the archangels would guide us better, make things more definitive, but now, all they can tell us is when you find yours, you'll know," Luc explained.

"That's cryptic," I replied. It made me think of a conversation I'd had with my mom about how to know when you're in love, when you've found the right person for you, your soul mate. She'd said pretty much the same thing. "You just know."

"Very cryptic." He waited patiently, watching while it all sunk in. I knew there was much more to it, but not sure how much more I needed to hear or could process anyway.

"How do those around you, friends, family, explain your all of a sudden being beamed up to Heaven?"

"People go missing all the time, sadly," Luc went on. "An accident, a runaway, an abduction or some angels just happen to be at a period in their lives where they're going to college or moving away, and no one hears from them again. With the state we leave our parents and those close to us in, sometimes they hardly notice. For some, it's a blessing."

"Some of the stronger human souls recover and become 'normal' again after the divine has been gone for a while. That's what we hope for anyway," Mo added.

~ ☾ ~

"Friends, classmates of guardians... are they affected like that too, with madness?" I started to panic.

"They can be, depending how close they get, how often they see the guardian angel, like if they play together daily from childhood, and see each other in school all the time. We try to keep exposure to a minimum. We move around a lot. Change schools. Stuff like that," Luc answered.

"So could I be in danger?" I straightened and pulled back from them.

Luc laughed. "It takes years. Years of being with us on a regular basis. My family didn't start showing real effects until I was 9 or so."

I relaxed slightly, and the three of us sat for several minutes in the dark horse field. Luc's eyelids were heavy and his eyes lined with dark circles. Mo's leg never stopped moving, jerking up and down. I took me a while to mull over everything they'd told me.

When it finally did, something occurred to me. I stood up suddenly, dusted myself off and said, "Right. I want you to talk to your archangels or whoever, and find out who the inept angel ass-hats were who killed me and my friends!"

Luc glanced to Mo before saying, "I don't think that's a good idea."

"Definitely not." Mo shook his head.

"I disagree. I want answers," I said.

"Lily, look, the angels in that situation are probably long gone by now," Luc said.

"Probably? Not if they didn't save the soul, right?" I asked. "What happens when your missions fail?"

"We aren't experts on this," Luc said. "Each guardian gets one soul to save, one mission or task at a time."

"Right."

"Once that is accomplished, the guardian returns home..."

~ ☾ ~

"Immediately?"

Luc again looked to Mo, who sat quietly, letting Luc do all the talking. "As I've never witnessed one myself I can only tell you what I've heard, but yes, it is immediate."

"I see. And if they fail?"

He exhaled heavily. "If they fail, which doesn't happen often, but has been known to, an investigation is begun into the incident."

"Investigation?"

"Yes, by the High Council to see if there was wrongdoing, to see if it could be helped, to see if the guardian in question had fallen or in the process of…" He took another deep breath. "If there was no wrongdoing or negligence, the guardian is reassigned."

"If there was?"

"It depends, Lily."

"If the angel had fallen…?"

"How familiar with the Bible are you?" he asked, answering my question with a question.

"Hell?" I asked.

"Something like that."

They again sat silently for some time. I paced the darkness of the field, lit only by the moon at this point. Mo sat cross-legged and arms folded, looking as though he wished he could close himself off from this conversation. He glanced nervously at Luc every time Luc answered another one of my questions. Luc sat defeated, knees up to his chest, nothing of his typical smirk or glint in his eyes. He just looked… done.

"So the angels who were assigned to save my friends…" I started again, focused.

"Lily, guardians don't always save souls by keeping people from dying," Luc tried to explain. "I mean, often that's the case, to keep people from harm, but clearly, if we kept everyone from dying, the world would be rather overcrowded, don't you think?"

"But they were so young," I said.

"True. We're often sent to save the lives of those who are young and innocent because it's not their time. Sometimes it's about something else entirely."

"How so?"

"Well," he began, "sometimes we save someone from temptation, sometimes we put people back on the right track in their life, sometimes we keep people from making mistakes or getting involved with evil people... It can be any number of things. Our primary goal is to preserve a soul, so it remains pure. I'm not sure how else to explain it."

"In mint condition," I supplied the answer.

"So to speak, and in some situations the obvious solution is just to keep the soul alive."

"But not always," I tried to understand.

He shook his head. "Not everyone has their own guardian angel."

"Why not?" I asked.

"They just don't."

"What, they aren't as important as those who do?" I asked. I glared at him.

Luc shrugged. "They just may not be destined to be anything more than the soul they are. Some souls have one shot. They lead a simple life. They're happy or they're not. They just aren't destined for more."

I frowned at this answer. What if my friends just weren't deemed important enough to have their own angels?

Mo spoke up. "You need to ask her about... the other thing." He gestured to the spot where Mike had appeared before.

"About what?" I asked.

"Before... you were talking to someone," he eased into it.

~ ☾ ~

"Mike," I answered.

"How did you see him? How did he appear to you?" Luc pressed.

"I was just out here, and he spoke to me."

"He spoke to you? Or you called to him?" Luc asked

I thought about it. "I was talking to myself, and he answered. Why?"

"Because we saw him, too. He was right there speaking to you."

"I know. I guess lately anything seems possible," I responded.

"Yes but that's not generally how it works. It's not like how it is in movies and TV. Psychics and séances can't contact the dead. Once people have passed, they don't appear and talk with those left on earth. There are rules about all of it, about how and who guardians can talk to, a chain of command so to speak. Once souls have crossed over, they go through a process."

"What kind of process?"

"Luc, I think this is really too much information for her," Mo interjected.

Luc nodded. "Let's just say the soul is busy. A soul wouldn't be able to fit it in his or her agenda to go back to Earth for a meeting. Sometimes doing so would be very painful, and sometimes a soul would get confused or decide to stay…"

"Like ghosts?" I asked.

"Yes."

"But it is possible?"

"It is, but extremely rare."

I laughed. "I didn't make it up or imagine it. You saw him too, otherwise, I would have thought it was a dream or a breakdown."

"I know. We aren't sure what to make of it. First God's silence and now things like this are happening." Luc tangled his fingers in his hair again.

~ ☾ ~

"We are seriously out of the loop when it comes to celestial matters right now," Mo explained.

"Maybe you should try to talk with your boss. Can you do that?" I pushed.

The two of them looked at one another again, trying to gauge how much of their big secret to tell. Then they nodded.

"So do it and I want to be there to ask about my friends."

"No, Lily, no. Absolutely not. I've already revealed too much to you. I've put myself, my mission, my team in danger in doing so. It's best left alone."

I could tell arguing with him wouldn't do any good at this point. A yawn took hold of me, and I realized it was late. I rubbed my hands up and down my arms to fend off the cold.

"Fine," I said.

"You're trembling. Look, it's late… or early. I've given you a lot to digest. Why don't you go home, get some sleep, and we can talk later. I'm sure you'll have more questions." Luc took off his army flak jacket and put it over my shoulders. I felt his body heat on it and never wanted to give it back. Butterflies began to stir inside me. I hadn't even realized I'd been shaking.

Mo stood and dusted off his jeans. "Aren't you grounded too? You're going to be in so much trouble!"

I smiled weakly at him, grabbed my backpack and allowed them to walk me back toward my house. We walked in silence most of the way, while the gears were spinning like crazy in my head. Eventually we stopped at my driveway. Before they got their good-byes out, I asked one more thing that had been bothering me. Something Luc had talked about in the theater earlier.

"So you guys and the juniors, all guardians…all being in one place… means something bad is going to happen, doesn't it?"

~ ☾ ~

They both tensed.

Luc answered after what seemed like an eternity. "Probably something very bad."

26 Road Trip

    I hardly slept that night. Everything ran through my head on a continuous loop, and I couldn't seem to calm down. As usual, I couldn't deal with school when I woke up, but I needed to see them… the guardians, now that I knew what they were. Maybe more of them would talk to me and give me answers, Belle or some of the juniors. My reporter instinct kicked in, and I wanted to interrogate them all, get quotes, and hear their version of things.
    I wondered how many of them had spoken to God before His silence, how often they spoke to their archangels, how many of them had found their souls, what happened to them next when they returned back home.
    All of these questions and more ran through my head, as did the most important one…. What had happened to the guardians who were supposed to protect Julie and Mike? Didn't two innocent kids deserve guardians? Had theirs fallen or had they just failed?
    What about me? I'd been saved. Was it just luck, like my minister had said? Did I have a guardian? Where were they now, Heaven? Maybe Luc and Mo knew them? Why would I have been brought back, but Julie and Mike hadn't? What was so great about me?
    Too curious for my own good, I pulled into the school parking lot, as dozens of others were doing, turned off the car, and watched all of the people walking inside the building. I wondered if any of them were guardians. Were any of them a soul in danger who needed saving?

~ ☾ ~

Were any of them the evil influence here to corrupt the innocent? Were any of them the reason for the catastrophe to come?

The more the questions came, the less I wanted to stick around to find out what the great disaster was or to learn whether I was one of the souls on the chopping block again. I'd already died once. I needed answers to all of the questions surrounding the accident. I had to find out what had really gone on and why.

I saw everything with new eyes and wanted to go back and view the accident site with a new understanding. I started the car but before I put it in reverse, Luc climbed in the passenger seat.

He didn't say anything, just buckled his seat belt and looked at me.

"Luc, what…?" I started to ask.

He flashed me a sad version of the smirk that had given me butterflies so many times before. "I know where you're going, and I'm going with you."

"You do?" How could he? I'd only figured it out a minute ago. Oh right, divine being.

"Yup, let's find out what happened to your friends' angels — and yours." He faced forward, waiting for me to drive.

I nodded and put it in gear. The old me had flashes of panic… I was skipping school again, my parents didn't know, I should tell someone, but the new me with the perspective of everything going on and how it all really worked had taken over. There was gas in the tank, a cell phone charger in the car, an angel sitting next to me, what did I have to lose? Other than notes in LA3 and the respect of Mr. Potter.

So I drove while Luc fiddled with the radio station.

"Do you know where you're going?" Luc casually asked me.

"Not really. The crash site maybe?"

~ ☾ ~

"What do you expect to find?"

"Not sure. Why don't you just ask your bosses what the scoop is? Save us the trip?"

"I'm all about the trip." He smirked. Light shone behind him through the window as the sun rose higher in the sky, making him appear to glow.

"You could make this a lot easier."

"Not really. The archangels aren't at liberty to discuss every soul saving process that goes on. It would take a lot of bookkeeping to keep straight." I could see his grin from my peripheral vision.

"You're making fun of me? Angels do that? Tsk tsk." I shook my head. "Well I don't know how these things work. I just know I need to find answers."

"I've given you too many answers as it is. But I will try to help you understand, and I feel compelled to also defend the guardians you're looking for."

"Why?"

"Because I'm a guardian. I understand the job, and especially now with the silence, I understand how hard it is to achieve. If your friends' angels fell or failed or didn't recognize their souls, I completely understand."

I narrowed my eyes and turned toward him.

"I'm not saying it's okay, but it is understandable. Maybe they didn't fail after all," he added.

"How can that be possible? How is letting two young and innocent people die suddenly not a failure?" He just shrugged. "Do you know how much it destroyed everyone? Do you know how much suffering that left in its wake?"

"I can only imagine. But we aren't to question the big game plan. Sometimes suffering leads to change... positive change."

"I won't accept that as an answer."

"Lily, people always pray and ask, 'if there is a God, why is there so much suffering in the world? Why are there earthquakes that kill thousands? Why are innocent babies born with crack addictions or AIDS?'"

"We aren't supposed to question God, yadda yadda yadda. I know."

"That's the answer we're supposed to give, but the answers are all there, right in front of you."

"What's that supposed to mean?" I asked, looking at the highway before me.

"You've read the Bible."

"Parts."

"You know the stories… Noah, Abraham, Adam & Eve, the serpent."

"So?"

"So some things are tests. Some things happen to clear out the corruption—"

"So my friends were killed to clear out corruption? Or they were a stupid test? For who, their parents?"

"I don't know, Lily. Maybe for you."

I hit the brakes and my Chevy fishtailed. Dust billowed behind us as I ran it along the side of the road, barely staying out of the ditch. I regained control and stopped.

"For me? They died for me? This is my fault?" I looked him right in the eyes, too upset to get distracted by the endless green.

"I didn't say it was your fault, Lily. But look how their deaths have changed your life." He held my hand.

I thought about what he said. The accident had changed my life. I moved to my dad's, new school, new life. I'd suffered depression and contemplated suicide…

"Think about how much you've changed. How strong you are, how unafraid."

Unafraid? Was I unafraid or did I just not care anymore?

"Plus their deaths led you to… us." The pause made me think he was about to say "*to me*" but he stopped

~ ☾ ~

himself. "You may not buy into it, but everything really does happen for a reason. You have died, been to Heaven and then moved a few hundred miles away to land right smack in the middle of a cluster of angels. Do you think it's just coincidence? Not only that, but the accident shifted the direction of your life. Maybe, just maybe, your life would have headed down the wrong track if you remained behind, and now you're somewhere else."

"My life has felt pretty derailed since."

"Look, I don't know if that's the reason, but I'm just throwing it out as a possibility. By the way that event didn't just change you, it changed others as well." He searched my face carefully. "How can I explain this? Sometimes good things come out of tragedies. Take a forest fire for example. The entire forest appears destroyed, devastated, but the underbrush is cleared out and actually cleanses everything to allow for better re-growth."

"After a horrible winter," I said, helping him, "spring returns."

"Exactly, and sometimes, like when a parent loses a child, say to abduction, they make it their life's work to change laws and pass initiatives and start groups to help find other missing children."

"So the child is a sacrifice? A pawn that has to suffer for the greater good?"

He paused a long time, and took a deep breath before responding thoughtfully, "Sometimes, Lily, the child is the guardian."

Those words hit me with a force which would have knocked me over had I not been already sitting. I needed some air. I got out of the car and started walking in the tall grass on the side of the road. I heard his car door open behind me.

He didn't say anything, but let me walk it off. I'm not

sure how long I wandered in the field by the highway, but eventually I made my way back to the car. Luc waited on the hood of my beige Chevy, holes in his jeans, forearms resting on his knees. The sun had risen behind him and shone through his shaggy hair. All this time I knew I'd been crushing on him, but looking at him with his bright green eyes and his sly smirk, I knew I loved him.

When I looked in his eyes, I couldn't turn away. It was like some stupid magical connection; when our eyes met I could read him. I knew what he thought and felt and knew he wasn't just good, but pure, genuine, perfect. I felt the warmth and knew he loved me. "I know," I said, probably not making any sense.

I couldn't read minds or anything, but I could read Luc and knew he could read me. There was a link between us, and I longed to be with him every minute of every day. It was love in a sense I'd never experienced before. I was so confused about him at first, and it had scared me and kept me away. I wasn't used to being touchy feely or making eye contact. I'd felt safer hiding behind my wall of hair, letting it block my view and keep everyone at a distance, especially since the accident.

But now, after talking with him and spending time with him, I knew what the feeling was. I could label it; name it and face it rather than hide from it. I loved Luc.

I loved everything about him. I loved the holes on the insides of his dirty black Converse All Stars. I loved his careless army flak jacket frayed at the cuffs. I loved the shape of his fingers. I loved his grin and his eyes and his shoulders. I couldn't compare him to any other person or divine being. The intense feeling washed over me, obliterating the butterflies and making me feel whole, healed, restored.

I needed to be near him, his presence… so I walked slowly up to him. He looked at me strangely since I didn't slow as I got to him. He straightened, but I moved until I closed in on him. I took his face in my hands and kissed him like I'd never kissed anyone in my life, as though my life depended on it, all the while knowing he could be gone tomorrow and we had no stable future together. All we had was the moment and the kiss. Love lit me up until I felt like I was brighter than the sun behind him, and finally... finally for the first time since I'd died, I felt alive again.

He put his hands up to stop me at first in a feeble attempt at best. Slowly his tension released and his body relaxed as he kissed me back. I felt like I was home. The kiss was light and innocent and sweet. It was pure and all encompassing. I didn't feel the usual guilt for being happy. I didn't feel sad for living. The kiss mended everything.

Flashes from the accident zipped through my brain at super speed, the crash, drowning, death. The images slowed when I got to the white space, the feathery space. Heaven. Hope. Happiness. All I'd felt when I'd been dead shot through me again. A release. A letting go. Peace. The rush of divinity didn't scare me this time. Nothing scared me in Luc's arms.

I pulled back, reluctantly. Luc's eyes were wide with wonder.

"I'm your guardian. I wasn't before, when you had the accident. But from the first time I saw you walk by the drama classes, I knew. I've always known it was you. You're my soul," he said. Yet he still sat on the hood of my car, right there in front me. I felt healed by him. My problems were solved, the clouds were clearing, and somehow I knew he could feel it too. Happiness flowed through me for the first time since before I'd died, pulsating through my veins like another heartbeat. True happiness.

"I know," I answered, smiling up at him. We got back

~ ☾ ~

in the car and just sat there for a long time, letting it sink it. My mind reeled from all of it. After a while, I went back to what he'd said about the child earlier. "Sometimes the child is the guardian," I repeated.

He nodded.

"And my friends?"

"Mike came to you after his passing," he explained. "Like I said, it just doesn't happen the way the psychics would like you to think. Souls of those who've died don't return like that."

"But angels do. He was a guardian," I said and smiled fondly, remembering Mike. I'd loved him, not quite the way I loved Luc. What was it with me and angels? There had always been something in Mike's eyes, too. Had he known who his soul was? Had he spoken to God?

"I think he was," he answered.

"What about Julie?"

"I don't know. Maybe she was the soul he saved?"

"Can we find out?" I tried to keep the desperation out of my voice.

"Lily, I know you want answers." He lightly brushed my face with the back of his hand. "But there are some things you may never know. Maybe Mike did save Julie, by just being with her in the end, so she didn't die alone. Maybe he helped her pass to the next life. This guardian stuff, there are things we only find out once we've completed our mission, and then we're gone." He stopped short, his brows furrowed.

"Right now, after being with you. I feel—" I didn't know how to explain it. "I feel better. Like at peace. I think you just saved me... with a kiss... how Grimm's Fairy Tales of you." I poked him in the ribs to get him to laugh, but he didn't.

He started looking around frantically, as though waiting for something to happen, and he clutched my hands tightly. "Yes, I... don't understand."

~ ☾ ~

"What is it, Luc?"

He got out of the car and scanned the horizon, the meadow on the side of the highway, the clouds above.

"You're still here." I clued in eventually.

"Something's wrong... something..." He closed his eyes and stood very still, concentrating. A minute or so passed before he opened his eyes again.

"The silence?" I offered getting out of the car.

"It can't be. When we save a soul, we go home." He sounded frantic, but I couldn't tell why. Was he that desperate to return?

"Is that so bad? I mean, that you haven't gone back?"

He calmed and looked at me, locking me with those eyes. "Yesterday, I would have said not returning would be tragic."

"And today?"

"Today, there is nowhere I'd rather be than with you. It just concerns me—"

"Why?" I asked.

"It just means... something's wrong. Either you're not saved yet, or there's a much bigger problem. Something isn't right with the system, for lack of a better word."

"If you haven't saved me yet, then don't. I'm fine. I mean, if I'm not saved yet, just let it go, and stay here with me," I urged.

He smiled sadly. "I don't know what's happening, but if you aren't saved, it's in my nature to protect you. I couldn't just *not* save you." His brow furrowed as he tried to explain. "It's the only thing I want to do."

"But I want you to stay," I said, trying hard not to whine.

"And I want you protected. We should go. I should let the others know. They still have their souls to think of." He got back in the car.

"What about Mo?" That stopped him. Mo, his best friend, his fellow guardian. Mo had feelings for me, but I

~ ☾ ~

knew I couldn't be with him, not now. And Luc? How could he face Mo now?

"He knows the job. Some things are out of our control. I'll deal with Mo."

I hoped Mo would be as understanding as Luc thought he would be.

Luc phoned the others as I drove him back, so they could gather for a meeting. I wasn't quite sure what he would tell them, how he'd explain our connection, but I believed he could handle it. He was so in charge when he spoke with them before.

He called the meeting in the theater, as usual. Seriously, where was this drama teacher anyway? Had she been touched by their proximity? It was mid-afternoon already; we'd been gone longer than I thought. The bell for the last period of the day was ringing when we returned, but classes never seemed to be an issue with them. Most of the other guardians, juniors included, were already in the theater when we arrived.

I walked hesitantly down the red-carpeted aisles of the theater with Luc. How could we explain this to Mo, would he know, would Luc do this in front of everybody?

Mo sat in the front row; some of the others were on the edge of the stage. Gregor lay across seats, apparently sleeping. When he saw us, Mo stood slowly, dramatically. Some of the juniors snickered, but Luc paid no attention and strode forward while I trailed nervously behind. When my eyes met Mo's, I'm sure I couldn't hide the guilt I felt. My face flushed.

"Good, everybody's here," Luc said.

"What the hell is this?" Mo asked, gesturing toward us.

"Not now."

"Yeah, now. Where have the two of you been?" he asked.

~ ☾ ~

Speak of the Devil

Tim chuckled. "Your absence was noted."

Hillary practically cackled. She might have beauty on the outside, but none on the inside clearly. Some angel she was.

"I wanted—" I started, but Luc held up a hand to stop me.

"Why is *she* here anyway?" Violet asked. "I thought this was a 'closed' meeting."

"She knows," Luc said.

"What?" I thought Hillary would choke on her own tongue, and kinda wished she would. I could think those things. *I* was no angel. Mo stood, fists clenched, glaring at the two of us.

"Quiet!" Luc commanded, holding up his hand while he waited for them all to settle. "Something isn't right."

Sean did a Darth Vader impression. "There's a disturbance in the force."

Tim stood next to Luc, representing the juniors. "Wait, let him talk."

"I've lost contact." He gave them all a pointed look, and I was clueless as to what he meant. He was still keeping important information from me.

The others reacted with alarm, glancing from one to the other. Gregor even sat up and paid attention. Tim nodded. "Same here — I tried to reach Rafe earlier. Nothing."

"Wai...wai...wait...wait a minute. What?" Mo asked. "How is that possible? We can't reach the archangels now either?"

Even I knew that wasn't good.

"I tried. No response. I think we need to be prepared," Luc said.

"For what?" Violet asked.

"For the inevitable. For the reason we're here."

As if on cue the fire alarm in the school start ringing.

~ ☾ ~

27 All Hell

Everyone jumped up wide-eyed, gripping the backs of the theater seats or diving to the floor to brace for some kind of impact. Sean started laughing. "Relax people. I'm sure it's a drill or a prank. Let's just move to the fire exits."

Over the PA system, the principal said, "Everyone please quickly evacuate the building in an orderly fashion, moving to your respective safe areas and check in with your teachers."

"That's strange," Mya noted. "Usually no one comes on the loud speaker to talk. We just scuffle out or sneak home. Something's not right."

Luc frowned. "Let's head to the ball field and finish this."

Some of them rose and put their backpacks on, heading out, but Mo wouldn't let it go. "Let's finish this right here!" He walked up to Luc and shoved him, hard.

"Mo!" I shouted and got between them.

"Awwww," Mo said, nasty and mocking. "Isn't this sweet?" He pushed me a bit too forcefully aside into one of the rows of seats. I flew gracelessly back and crumpled to the ground.

"Hey!" Belle leapt up, Matrix style, appearing from nowhere to stand in front of me.

Hillary cackled again and Sean laughed. *Nice angels*, I thought, and then panic hit me. What if they were no longer angels? I remembered everything I'd overheard in the theater. Tim thought Belle was gluttony, Violet envy, and Sean wrath. The seven deadly sins overcoming

~ ☾ ~

them. Were they all really falling? Was I surrounded by angels or demons?

Luc steadied himself before he lurched forward to Mo, grabbing his shirt and lifting him off his feet. "I said *not now*!"

Tim herded his guardians out, though Hillary nearly fell over backwards, trying to remain behind to watch when the school security guard came in.

"All right kids, out. Let's move. Quickly now," he instructed.

His walkie-talkie spit static and immediately came to life. "The bomb is on the lower level. We are working at disarm —" The security guy jolted to action, eyes bulging and fingers fumbling as he tried to silence the talkie before we could hear any more.

We all froze. "Did he say bomb?" Hillary asked, her voice steadily climbing into a shriek.

The security guy sighed but quickly moved into action. "Yes, now come *on*, out, out, *out*!"

Luc released Mo and immediately appeared at my side with his supernatural speed. He latched on to my arm, leading me out of the theater. The security guy did a double take but just shook his head and continued to usher them out.

"You heard the man. This is not a drill. This could be it folks. It's now or never." Though Luc tried to sound confident and in control, I detected a slight crack in his voice.

"But, if the connection is broken, how will we know?" A touch of hysteria tainted Violet's voice. "How will we find them? And if we save them, are we stuck here?" Mo took her arm the same way Luc had taken mine and guided her out the theater exit.

"All will be revealed," he said firmly. But we knew the truth; the truth was we just didn't know the answers to any of those questions.

~ ☾ ~

We walked out, calmly, trying not to trample one another, merging in the hallway with the rest of the school. But none of them had heard the walkie-talkie announcement to know about the actual bomb, so they were shuffling slowly, laughing and talking. They were screwed, and they didn't even know it.

I spotted a few of the guardians in the hall, but they were splitting up fast, spreading out through the crowd. Tim peered into the masses. "We have to save them all!" Cassie shouted, peeling away from the group.

"We can't, honey," Mya said, "But we can save our assigned soul."

"Like we know who that is," Kara sniped.

Belle, Gregor and even Sean, all of them I saw, searched through the swarm of students as if waiting for someone, but I knew they weren't sure who their someones were. My heart tightened in my chest in fear for all of us and pity for them. They so desperately needed to find their souls. The one soul who needed them was in this crowd somewhere, but where? Then there was Mo, helping Violet, though he turned back to watch me.

God, was I his soul to save? He sure thought so, and I had been drawn to him at first. I felt the warmth of Luc's grip on my arm. He held me firmly, not too tightly, but I knew it would take an act of God to get him to release me. I couldn't control who my guardian was any more than I could control who I loved. If feelings had anything to do with it, if they were some kind of clue or sign that pointed to my guardian, then Luc was definitely mine.

While we streamed toward the main exits through the crowds I couldn't help wonder what would happen when I was saved. Hadn't Luc saved me earlier? Like a fairy tale, his kiss had healed me, but Luc hadn't disappeared. Would Luc vanish before my eyes the instant my life lay

Speak of the Devil

wide open before me? It didn't seem fair. Wouldn't his leaving destroy me all over again? Would Mo be my guardian then? I laughed to myself. Was I so high maintenance I actually needed more than one angel to put me back together? Over and over again?

The high school, the middle school, and the elementary were all next to one another on the same street. As I saw daylight shining in from the exterior doors, something occurred to me. "Owen and Sophie." The realization hit me, but no one heard.

"Luc." I pulled my arm away and stopped walking, causing a bottleneck of congestion there in the doorway.

"Come on Lily!"

"Owen and Sophie," I said again.

He stopped and his face softened and he nodded. "Come on." He led me back to the theater against the flood of people exiting. "I know another way out." He maneuvered us out of the crowd.

If a bomb were in this building, what would happen to the other two? What domino effect would an explosion here have? Would they be safe?

He started moving even faster through the crowd wanting out, finally making some headway when the school exploded.

Just like in a movie, things happened frame by frame as if in slow motion. First a deep, rumbling roar came from behind and below me. It felt and sounded like it was coming from the school's basement boiler room. There was a buildup of pressure, then a loud crack, as if the elastic from a giant slingshot had snapped.

There was rumbling that wasn't just a noise; the floors shook and the building around us trembled and bucked under my feet. I grabbed Luc's arm and tried to steady myself. The broken school started flying everywhere. I held up my arm to cover my head and ducked down while Luc leaned over me. More rumbling

~ ☾ ~

followed by a loud moan, the sound of our school, its walls, its ceiling, its lockers, its glass trophy cases, bookshelves, desks, chairs, all of it scraping, blasting, crumbling, slamming, crashing around us, as if the school itself were in pain.

All I could think was, "This can't be happening, bomb scares are just threats. There's never really a bomb at the school!"

"Lily!" Luc shouted, pushing me down, shielding me from the shrapnel coming at me from all directions.

The school leaned and groaned as weakened beams slowly let go of their hold on the walls, and more crashing and destruction followed, triggering another weak wall to tumble. I felt the school shuddering around me like a frightened child, as I huddled beneath Luc.

My mind raced to all of those around me, those without guardians. Why didn't everyone have a guardian? What about Owen and Sophie? Did the other guardians find their souls? Flashes of everyone I knew at the school ran through my mind like a slideshow in the seconds of impact and chaos. Ms. McNair, Belle, Mr. Potter, Cassie...

Dust clouds and smoke formed in the air. I could barely breathe.

I flashed back to the accident. The darkness. The lack of oxygen. But the difference here was the noise. In the car there had been a muffled silence once I went under and a soft feel as water enveloped me. Here in the school the noise was overwhelming, battering my eardrums, louder than anything I'd ever heard before. More debris fell around us, and the ceiling overhead gave way and dumped a pile on top of Luc and me. Pain, things I couldn't even identify slammed into me, cutting and crushing. No soft blanket of water to ease me into the next life. This type of dying sucked. I felt the initial force and sharp slice, and everything went black.

~ ☾ ~

Speak of the Devil

***

I don't know how long I was unconscious. When I came to I saw I was clear of the pile and Luc had dug some of the others out of the debris. "Luc?" I choked and coughed, barely able to speak. He moved to me stepping over the piles of school. I noticed a door had been propped up to lean over me, shielding me from any more fragments that might fall.

"Ah, you're awake now. Just stay still for a minute. I'm helping some of the others. I checked you out, and you're okay. Just hold tight, while we dig through some of this stuff to find the best way out."

The exterior doors to the building were up ahead, or at least they had been. They had been blown away, choked with debris, and the glass that used to be the two story windows on either side lay blasted in pieces outside the doors. I saw the sun through the dust clouds and falling pieces of my school and watched as it settled down to touch the horizon. I must have been out of it for a while. The days were getting shorter but normally the sun didn't set while we were still at school.

I felt okay. My head hurt a little, but Luc had rescued me. As the dust settled it coated everything in a grim gray blanket, and falling parts of the school echoed around us. I tried to get up to see the wreckage.

I began to shake, shock stuttering my heart and giving me chills. I had been in an explosion. My school looked like it had been the center of a war zone. I tried to breathe in but dust or smoke choked me, and I started coughing. Other coughs echoed in the distance. The sound of people digging out broke the silence that followed the blast. Others were alive, but so much dust and detritus blocked our path, I couldn't see who.

"How are you feeling? You doin' okay?" Luc asked, desperation touching his voice.

"Relatively speaking."

~ ☾ ~

"Come on then." He reached down and helped me up. "Let's get you outside, so you can breathe."

I started coughing again and nodded. "What about the others? Is everyone okay?" I choked out through coughs. The school now smelled like dust and mildew rather than sweat socks and cafeteria sloppy Joes.

"I don't know." His voice sounded grim.

"Wait." I pulled him back to me. "You're still here."

"I know." He said nothing further, just motioned me to exit. As he walked ahead of me through the gaping hole in the school toward the sun sinking low on the horizon, I saw something. His silhouette wasn't that of a teenager. His silhouette had wings, and as he walked they spread out from him like a bird preparing to fly.

The guy I love is an angel, I thought. The warmth I felt earlier when we'd kissed rushed through me. I was happy even in the midst of the destruction and death around me. I knew it would be okay because Luc was there. Everything would be okay, from now on.

He turned. "Are you coming?" he asked. I simply stood there in awe, in shock. "Here." He came back and scooped me up. I lay weak and limp in his arms and put my arms around his neck as he carried me out of the cloudy, fallen building. A beautiful boy with amazing green eyes, a crooked smirk, and angel wings carried me to safety.

The dust settled and visibility improved. Making our way out didn't seem difficult for him; he climbed over the wreckage more easily than I would have been able to even on a regular day. I looked around and saw more of the damage, the important damage. I tightened my grip around his neck and gasped. The legs under the boards and glass, the bleeding limbs, the faces with fearful gazes that would never close on their own again. Why were these people taken while I'd been blessed with a guardian angel to protect me?

~ ☾ ~

"Lily," Luc said, in a tone he usually took with the other guardians, commanding and strong. "Look at me."

"Right." I nodded and tried to focus on him, angel wings and all. I locked gazes with him on purpose for once. As usual it was hard to see anything else. "Your wings. When did you get those? Are those your reward maybe?"

"My what?" He gave me a funny look.

"Your wings. Won't everyone see?"

We climbed our way toward the exit as sirens sounded in the distance. "No one can see my wings, Lil."

"I can." I reached out and stroked one. It felt like I imagined it would, soft, downy, feathers. His wing jerked under my fingers. He pulled back from me a little.

"You can? You can touch...?" I'd never seen him look so surprised.

"Guys!" a dust choked voice sounded behind us. I turned to see Belle carrying another student, his arm over her shoulders while she walked him out. Belle, too, had beautiful white angel wings, which flapped slightly as she carried this person out as if to help ease the load.

Luc didn't seem to react to Belle's wings, nor did the coughing student she carried out. Behind her, I saw more movement. I couldn't tell from this distance who was rising from the debris to make it toward the exit. Had I hit my head? Was I dreaming in some coma in a hospital somewhere or could I still be dead from the first time? No, I knew it was real.

Sirens blared in the distance. Help, mortal help, would be here soon, but I was awestruck, watching Luc and Belle. They were beautiful and glorious. Flashes shuttered through my mind of stained glass cathedral windows and cement statues at cemeteries. I'd known it but it hadn't completely sunken in, until now. Angels. From God. Here to save us.

Rumbles and crashes came from somewhere inside

~ ☾ ~

the school as Belle carried the student out. Settling dust plumed again to hang thick in the air when another wall came down, making breathing difficult. I pulled my t-shirt up over my nose and mouth to act as a filter.

"The building isn't stable. I have to get you outside!"

Right, I thought. Owen and Sophie. I had to get out to see what had happened to them.

Not many other people were making their way out. Through the ash and dust, there wasn't a lot of movement except for the random wall or shelving unit giving way, adding another crash to the others. Adding more dust clouds to the hallways.

He carried me to the doorway and gently set me on my feet once safely outside the remains of the building. I could hear sirens outside getting louder. Belle struggled towards the door, and Luc helped her get her injured student outside as well. The boy took my hand, and I guided him carefully through the door so he wouldn't get cut on the broken glass.

"Luc?" I heard Belle ask, her voice concerned.

I noticed they'd turned back toward the building. I thought nothing of it at first. Maybe they'd seen someone else who needed help, but then I saw the others coming. Mo, Hillary, and Sean. The sun slipped under the horizon, but before it did, at the moment where day and night kissed, I saw who they were, *what* they were.

Their wings were dark, and bony nubs appeared high on their foreheads. I blinked to clear my vision. Maybe it was the clouds of dust in the air making me see things. The three of them walked out; they weren't helping anyone and the air around them was dark. When I looked at Luc, light seemed to be backlighting him almost all the time. Either the sun was behind him or just a glow about him beamed from his smirky smile. With them there was almost a darkness, or at least an

~ ☾ ~

unsettling absence of light surrounding them. But even more disturbing were the red-black wings, like those of a bat with flesh stretched too thin between the bones they were sporting.

I protectively clung to the injured boy and backed away. Luc and Belle acted as shields between us and the fallen guardians, or whatever they were now. I tried to hurry the boy out on my own. He groaned, in pain.

"It's okay." I tried to comfort him. Then I saw the two people who'd helped me the most, the two with angel wings, the two who cared about me and I'd grown to care for despite all of the pain and emotion I'd tried to avoid feeling again. I saw them start to shimmer.

"Lily, go! Now!" Luc ordered.

"Saved your souls, did ya?" Mo asked, a sickening grin on his face.

"Luc?" Belle cried and took hold of his arm.

"Lily. Go!" Luc said and gave a quick look back at me. Our eyes met, and I remembered how I'd been so lost in them before. I could read them and knew what he was trying to tell me.

"No!" I protested.

"You got this, Lily." He smiled his casual smirk for me, but the smile didn't reach his eyes.

"Go on Lily," Mo added. "I'll catch up with you later." Hillary and Sean laughed.

Belle gave me a worried look, before turning to the others. "Leave her alone," she commanded.

"Look, your job here is done guys, right? Take off. We'll clean up the souls you leave behind," Sean said, giving me and the student I was propping up a look.

A shiver ran down my spine, and I knew I had to get this guy out of there, fast. Luc and Belle were shimmering harder.

"Good job. Tell the big guy — if He's around — we said hello."

~ ☾ ~

A flash of light so bright it dazzled me erupted before us. I shielded my eyes but saw a flurry of white wings and green eyes. The emptiness that followed deafened me.

I was barely able to see or hear, but I moved the barely conscious, innocent guy, the other saved soul, onto the grass. Muted laughter came from behind me, but I kept moving, trying to process what had happened.

"We're coming for you, Lily," Mo said fiercely. "And there is no one left to rescue you."

~ ☾ ~

28 Loose

I should be getting good at this, I thought. Just another pair of friends, gone, taken to Heaven, and me here left on earth to spiral out of control again. Just when I'd felt healed. Just when I'd begun to move on. At least I hadn't died this time.

I had no time for self-pity. Demons were closing in on me, and here I had to get this injured guy to safety. Lucky for him I was good with the auto-pilot mode. Luc's last words, "You got this," echoed in my head. *Put one foot in front of the other*. Each step got me closer to safety. I tried to tune out the demons out behind me, but heard Mo's laughter and Hillary's Evil Barbie screeching from time to time.

They could have been on me in seconds if they wanted to, but they seemed to enjoy scaring me. Mo and Sean in particular, knew me well enough to know what I'd just been through with Mike and Julie. They were probably pretty damn sure I was in shock. They were going to toy with me, bat me around like a cat does to a stunned mouse. I had to keep moving.

I got the guy out to the parking lot, past some stragglers outside. We weren't the first ones out of the school. Survivors, rescue teams and rubber-neckers were congregating in the parking lot. They started clapping as we came out. As if we'd done something special — all we did was stagger out of the wreckage.

An EMT from one of the ambulances ran over to help us. I zoned out a little, mesmerized by the spinning lights on top of the vehicles, trying not to flash back to

~ ☾ ~

that rainy night when I lay on the side of the road like a squashed raccoon. He took the boy and another medic started quizzing me.

"How did you get out?"

The words spun in my head like the ambulance lights. I flashed back to the accident and couldn't answer. Confusing the two momentarily. *The car ran off the road.* I stared at the flashing lights. *There was water. I couldn't breathe.* I remembered telling the deputies at the hospital after my accident.

Soon a police officer ordered spectators to move back while they put up yellow caution tape.

I can't remember what all they asked me. The blast had affected my hearing, so everything sounded muffled and slowed, drowned out by this horrible ringing. Once they had me seated me on the ambulance's tailgate, I felt safe enough to look back.

The back end of my school lay in shambles, a smoking, collapsed mess. That anyone had made it out alive was a miracle. Why? Me and miracles. Why me? I was nobody. A nothing from a broken family who'd never been a track star or a mathlete or anything spectacular. I wasn't destined to be Homecoming Queen. I was just a regular girl. Not beautiful. Not brilliant. Why did I keep getting saved? In the middle of all my questioning I realized the fallen angels, Mo, Sean and Hillary, hadn't followed me out. Lucky for me because I just sat there on the back of the ambulance doing nothing and being nothing. I stared at the blown out back entrance of the school and watched as slowly more people trickled out.

The paramedic said something else to me. I just shook my head and pointed, like a toddler who hadn't learned to speak yet. "Back there, Luc and Belle..." *Mike and Julie.* "The others are coming. My brother and sister!" I was babbling. I'm sure the EMT thought I was

~ ☾ ~

in shock or had a head injury. He finally just told me to relax and not to talk.

He went back into the ambulance to get something for me, but I had to find Owen and Sophie. I could see the bulk of their buildings from where I sat, and they were intact, but all of them had been evacuated, too. There were hundreds of students slowly meandering to the football field.

I didn't think they were in danger from the explosion anymore, but there were demons on the loose. One in particular wanted to hurt me and would know where to find my siblings. I jumped up and ran to the elementary school before the EMT could stop me. Immediately the pain in my knee registered.

"You got this, Lily." One foot in front of the other. Push the pain out. Find Owen and Sophie. Keep them safe. If I thought about anything else I was lost. But every now and then my mind would wander... did all of the guardians save their souls? Were the only ones left the fallen and the failures? What did they want?

Luc hadn't shared everything he knew. Some things had remained sacred, but it would have been nice to know the details. We'd never talked about what would happen after he'd been beamed back up. Was it permanent? Would I ever see him again?

One foot in front of the other. Tears streamed down my face as I limped as fast as I could to the elementary school. The alarms in the school were going off in a loud ring. Some of the littler kids were holding their ears, others cried. I had to find Sophie. Unfortunately, I had been a pretty self-absorbed older sister. I didn't know her teacher's name, so I rushed through the crowds, frantically searching for her and calling out her name. There were over two hundred elementary students crowded in clumps outside of the building overlooking the smoking ruins of the high school. Luckily, most of

~ ☾ ~

them were too small to realize what that meant for many of their older siblings. I caught a glimpse of it and half the building had survived. The theater half was a burned out shell. How anyone could have survived…

"Sis? You're okay!" Owen shouted to me from the other side of a sea of little kids. He had Sophie in tow. He'd been a better older sibling than me and made it to her first. I wiped away tears of relief, wading through the small kids to get to them. I scooped both up in a huge bear hug.

"You're okay!" I held back waves of sobs. I didn't want to upset them.

"Us?" Owen gave a subtle motion back toward the high school Sophie wouldn't catch. "I was worried about you."

I glanced down the hill at my school. New clouds of dust were rising lit by rescue crew floodlights, which meant more of the walls were falling. More people were probably dying, or having their souls taken. I knew this should affect me more, but it seemed so surreal I couldn't get my head around it. On any given day having your school explode would be shocking. Having also been rescued by an angel and chased after by demons? It felt like a dream.

I had no idea what the fallen would do. How would they take someone's soul? It had to be the opposite of saving one, didn't it? Were they killing survivors? I didn't know.

I thought of those still left behind. Had Mr. Potter made it out? McNair, the flakey drama teacher who never seemed to teach? Mr. Black? Most of my friends were guardians, so either they had saved their souls and were already back home or they'd fallen and were creating havoc in the wake of the explosion.

"Sis?" Owen brought me back. "You are okay, aren't you? I mean, that's a dumb question." He knew people

~ ☾ ~

had died in the explosion, I could see it in his face. "You're not hurt though."

"She's limping," Sophie said all sweetness and innocence. Oblivious to the crumbling building just down the hill.

"I'll be okay. Let's just get out of here." I started wondering how we could. The parking lot was crowded with emergency vehicles and now press vans with camera crews blocked most of the exits. I even heard a helicopter above. My car was in the middle of all of it.

"I checked Sophie out with her teacher already." He was growing up so much and had this much more in hand than I did.

I nodded and we made our way to the junior high. After signing him out, we started back down the hill to the high school, to my car. "We should call the parents," Owen suggested. I looked at him, not quite following. "If they're watching the news, they're probably losing it right now."

"Good one." My phone had been on silent, a habit I had upon entering the school. When I took it out to call, I had eighteen missed calls. Most were from them. Two were from Mo. And one from Luc. I froze.

"Give it here." Owen took the phone from me and quickly called our parents.

I'd seen enough to know Luc's was the earliest one, from before school this morning. One from Mo had been shortly after, while his other one had been only a few minutes ago. *We're coming for you, Lily.*

You got this, Lily. Really? Do I really? Had Luc believed that? Because it seemed to me my thirteen-year-old brother had things much more in control than I did. Demons were coming, and I had no idea what to do.

One foot...

Owen handed my phone back. "They're good now. How are you going to get your car out?" There would be

~ ☾ ~

no easy way to get the car out of that confusion. Not to mention, Mo would expect me to go to my car. Demons were probably swarming it as we spoke.

More people streamed slowly from the building's opposite side, since the blast had been concentrated on the theater side, where we'd been. Others escaped safely out of the side closest to the highway. I had to wonder, *had the theater side been targeted*?

I hadn't answered Owen. My ears were ringing. I was suffering from information overload. It was like fifty people were talking to me at once, and I couldn't hear any of them clearly, but really it was just him. My own thoughts and the words of Mo and Luc were spinning in my head. I couldn't sort out what to focus on or deal with.

"This way." Owen led us around the exterior of the parking lot.

"No. Don't take us to my car," I said.

"I'm not. We're going for pizza. The folks can pick us up here. We can calm down, and best of all…eat!"

I smiled at my funny little brother, and limped my way across the empty lots behind the schools as we cut across to the pizza place.

I did everything I could not to cry as we seated ourselves inside. Owen knew enough to be freaked out but played it cool for Sophie. She didn't need the stress or the seriousness of what just happened to sink in.

Mario's Pizza was empty except for the waitress and the cook in the back. The TVs hanging in the corners of the large rectangular room were usually there to show sports shows, but now they were on the news. I could see images of my smoking pile of school on screen with lots of words scrolling along underneath it. Both of the pizza place employees were glued to the TV and hardly noticed our appearance.

Owen cleared his throat loudly to get the waitress's attention.

~ ☾ ~

"Sorry, hon!" she hurried over. "Have you seen this? It's so—"

"We've seen it," he said, cutting her off. "Up close and personal. Can we get some ice water stat, please?" He gestured not so subtly to me.

"Oh my Lord in Heaven!" She jumped back, like I might cause the pizza joint to explode, too. "Right away!" She scurried off.

"I must look bad," I said and tried to smooth my hair.

"You look a little horrible," Sophie said then smiled.

"Only a little? I guess that's something." I almost laughed. Her smile was contagious.

"I wouldn't worry about how you look. No one is here and if they were, you're excused." He stopped and looked at me. "Although maybe you should look at some of those cuts."

"You're kinda dirty," Sophie added.

"I'll go clean up."

I turned on the cold water in the bathroom and rinsed off my hands, which were filthy. Then I got up the courage to look at my face. Also filthy, as was my messed up hair. It stuck out all over the place with bits of school in it. I tried to pick them out as much as I could and washed the blood from my face, hands and knees. The jeans were a shredded mess at my knees, and my right knee was bleeding and swollen. I think I'd sprained my right ankle too. I took a deep breath.

Do not cry, I told myself. Crying doesn't fix things. Be strong. *You got this, Lily. Deep breaths. One foot in front of the other.* I kept running the mantras through my head. How would I survive losing Luc? On the other hand, how could I possibly be broken after being loved by him?

I can't explain what happened next but though I hadn't heard or seen anything, I sensed her presence, a divine presence with me. Electricity hit the air around me, like a cold static. I spun around hoping to see Luc.

"Lily." Violet put her hand on my shoulder. Her crazy hair seemed even crazier than normal.

I tensed immediately. "Violet."

"I know what happened." She sounded almost gentle, sympathetic. Something was wrong. Violet was never... nice.

I quickly snatched up a piece of glass I'd pulled from my hair a few minutes ago. "You're with them! Get away from me!"

"I'm not. I swear to you." Her eyes looked sincere.

"Ha, right. Like demons don't lie?" I eyed her closely. Violet had scrapes and bruises, like I did, but I saw no signs of the demon nubs or horns I'd seen on the other three. Nor did I see wings, white or blood red.

She sighed. "If I wanted to hurt you or take you, I could have done it by now."

This rang true, so I lowered my glass shard.

"I want to help you and whether you believe it or not, it's the truth," she said.

She turned to the sink and washed her hands and face, as if it didn't matter to her whether I believed her. Really, she had the upper hand. She had all of the guardian knowledge I didn't. She would know how to fight the fallen. She may even know how to get Luc back. Or at least if it was even possible.

I had no choice but to hear her out.

She continued to wipe the smears of blood off her face and hands, but I noticed when she did so, there were no cuts or abrasions underneath.

"Fast healing," she explained.

"You bleed?"

"Yes, we bleed at first, but we heal quickly and we can heal ourselves and others at times."

I raised my eyebrows at her. "Well?"

"Oh God," she said to me then smacked herself in the

forehead. "Sorry!" she said, looking up. "Wherever you are," she muttered. "Now let me rephrase. I may have overstated things a little..." She looked at the scratches on my face, head and arms, and held her palm over them. She closed her eyes and scrunched up her face for a second. My injuries tingled briefly but then disappeared.

"Minor healing," she went on. "The big stuff we can't do yet... as guardians. That's more archangel territory." She squatted down to get a better look at my knee and sucked in some air. "Yeah, that I can't do a lot for. I can make it and your ankle not hurt for a while, but those may give you trouble for a while." She held her hand to them again, closing the open wounds, but they were still sore underneath. "We have limitations."

"How do I stop Mo?" I asked getting right to the point.

She jumped up to sit on the counter of the bathroom. "Can you fight?"

I laughed. "A demon? Umm, no."

"It's not simple even if you could. You need certain things...."

"Silver bullets? Salt? Cold iron?" I watched a lot of TV. *Buffy, Supernatural.*

"Something like that. It's hard with demons, and I've never rolled with them before. All I know is lore and rumors."

"Let's hear some."

"What, like exorcisms and that sort of thing?"

"Can he possess me? Is that something I should be concerned about?" I was way out of my depth here.

"He could, but I don't think that's what he wants with you. Well it is, but not as in him taking over your body. He wants to possess you in another sense."

"What sense?" I was so freaked out I wasn't sure I wanted to know.

~ ☾ ~

Someone knocked softly on the door. "You okay in there, sis?" My little brother acted so much like a big brother to me I felt guilty.

"Yeah, Owen. I'll be right out. Trying to comb out this mess of hair."

It seemed to appease him.

Again Violet took a deep breath. "He wants to turn you."

"Turn me? Like a vampire or something?"

"Very much like. If he can get you to go bad, you'll be his. Luc wouldn't want you anymore."

"Luc! You say that like it's a possibility, but I saw him and Belle… I saw them shimmer and shine out of here, back to home base."

Violet paused, pinching the bridge of her nose as though fighting a migraine. "All I can say is it's not like he's dead."

"No? Then what's it like?"

"He and Belle saved their souls. Mission complete. So they returned home."

"Can Luc come back?"

"It's not that easy—"

"But you're not saying it's impossible?" She shook her head but didn't make eye contact.

"What do we do with Mo and the others?" I asked.

"Kill them." Violet stared into the mirror, eyes glazing over.

She looked away suddenly, like a dog hearing something off in the distance. "We have to move. Grab the kiddos and come with me!"

~ ☾ ~

29 Running

I grabbed some bread sticks on the way out and noticed Owen throw some bills on the table as he quickly chewed the food in his mouth. Before he could open it to speak, I cut him off.

"No time to explain. Follow us!"

Violet was hard to keep up with. She had preternatural speed and all, plus I had to make sure Owen and Sophie were keeping up.

"Don't look now. Keep moving," she shouted over her shoulder, making it almost impossible *not* to look. From behind us I heard glass smashing and car alarms sounding. "Almost there," she coached.

We made it to her car, a black Pontiac, and quickly buckled in as she sped off. I waited patiently for an explanation but got none.

"What the heck?" Owen finally piped up from the back seat.

"I'm giving you a ride home," she said.

"I was enjoying a triple cheese pizza!"

"There are more pressing matters."

"Violet, Owen and Sophie. Owen and Sophie, Violet." I cut through the pleasantries. "Now what?"

"In front of the kidlets?"

"Hey! I resemble that remark!" Owen protested again.

"Whatever your 'rules' will allow." She caught my meaning.

"Let's take the kids home, and I'll explain. Back there, though, the uhhhh others were getting close. Mo, in particular, is after you, but doesn't seem to mind taking a leisurely pace so he can destroy and create havoc along the way."

"Great." The sky was completely dark now, so I needed to get Owen and Sophie home. What I'd do after that, I hadn't a clue.

"Here." Violet pushed my arm off the center console between the front seats and raised it up. "There are two Celtic cross necklaces in there," she explained, keeping her eyes on the road. I rummaged around until I found them. "Give them to the kids." I did as she asked.

"Like vampires? Really?"

"The fallen don't like them. Not exactly like vampires. More like garlic to vamps. Crosses will repel them, not burn them or destroy them. Crosses are reminders."

"Reminders?"

Violet took a deep breath. "You already know way too much and it makes you an even bigger target." She tried to speak in a low voice, but I knew that probably just made Owen want to listen in more. "Even if we haven't had direct contact… with…"

"Your boss," I helped.

She nodded once and continued. "We guardians all know He exists. There is no questioning it for us." She paused.

"His existence isn't a question because we work for Him and have spoken to Him or to those who have at one time or another. There just are times when He's away on business for long trips and we wonder if He's coming back.

"The pendants are gifts from the boss and will remind the fallen of His presence. When they see those, they feel a twinge of guilt. Some of them, who haven't fallen hard, may turn back to being a guardian. Cases are rare but have been known to happen."

"So they're safe now then?" I asked, referring to my sibs.

~ ☾ ~

"They're better. I only had two, but there's nothing special about them. Any cross necklace or other piece of jewellery will work. Silver works better. Vamps again sort of thing."

I tried to mentally inventory my jewellery box at home. Being anti-religion lately didn't contribute to any silver cross collections.

"You were going to tell me about Luc..."

"Right." Another deep breath. "We aren't from here, but are assigned here, you know? He just went back home. Once he's there a few different things may occur. He could, worst case, be punished for violating rules or not acting in a manner befitting a guardian."

"What? Why?"

"I'm not saying I think it's likely. I'm just laying it out there for you. On the other hand, he may be promoted."

"Archangel?"

She nodded once. "And last, he may be reassigned."

"Back here? To Earth?" I asked, a little too loudly and a little too excited.

"I don't know what the heck you two are talking about," Owen interrupted, "but it sounds like you both hit your heads! Maybe you should see a doctor."

"Yes," she ignored him, addressing me. "But he may be assigned to China, South America, or the North Pole."

I understood. Him being reassigned didn't necessarily mean I'd ever see him again. "Would he start all over?"

"Be reborn? Not necessarily. Sometimes that's the punishment. Sometimes it's what's required of the mission. It just depends."

I cracked the window slightly for some fresh air and asked the next question very softly, fighting the break in my voice. "Would he... remember me?"

"Most likely. Even if he were reborn. We maintain our memories. All of us that you knew were on our first missions, so we were born into it. Doing it that way helps acquaint us with the human condition and all of that. We appreciate you all the more and you know… stuff. A second assignment doesn't require it in most cases. We remember everything. It helps us learn and grow."

I exhaled, relieved. Soon after we pulled into my dad's driveway and let the kids out. The house looked safe enough and unharmed. We had an alarm system my dad was vigilant about. I felt relatively okay with leaving them there, as long as I drew the baddies away.

I hugged them both. "Keep those necklaces on for good luck."

Owen made a face. "They're kinda weird."

"Tuck them under your shirt if you have to, but keep them on. For me, until I tell you otherwise."

He was a bright kid and knew from the snippets he'd heard of our bizarre conversation that something was up and it had to somehow do with the school explosion.

"But where are you going?" Sophie asked, rubbing her eyes.

"With my friend. I'll be back later."

I sat quietly as the car idled in the driveway, watching to make sure my siblings had walked the pathway to the house and entered unmolested. Once they were safe my head fell back against the head rest.

Violet put it in reverse and drove off.

"I have nothing left," I said. "I don't know how to help or get through this or why you're helping me." Violet didn't respond and I continued to babble on as though I'd been drinking. "I mean you, of all people. You've been a royal bitch since day one. What kind of angel are you anyway?"

I turned toward her to see her face lit by the electronics on the dash of her car. She drove on, showing no emotion on her face. After a few minutes of silence, I leaned back against the seat. I felt like slipping

~ ☾ ~

into apathy mode again, like I had after Julie and Mike, as if it were a warm, thick sweater on a cool day. But she broke the silence.

"A bad one," she finally answered. "One who didn't rescue her soul, and has to live with that knowledge and wonder.... Who was I supposed to save? Did I pass by their limbs sticking out from beneath the rubble when I saved my own skin after the blast? Did I hear their screams and turn my back on them to escape? Is my soul still out there waiting to be saved somewhere?"

That made me feel like crap. "I'm sorry. Look—"

"Until the explosion, this was all a game to me. Woooo, look at me! I'm a guardian angel with super powers. I'm super cute, super-fast, super strong. The family in the home I came into became more and more distant, echoing the family I had from home." She made an upward motion toward Heaven, and her voice started to crack.

"We lost touch with the big guy upstairs. Our archangels, the ones who look after us, were becoming less and less communicative while they dealt with whatever was going on above them. My friends were slipping away. It seemed less and less real to me, so I started to enjoy living like a human teenager.

"I had it all, right? Cute and powerful... divine. So much divinity within me I could drive men mad if I were around them too long." She laughed, though she didn't sound at all happy. "Literally.

"To top it all off, I was drawn to the other guardians. They were all attractive people with powers and abilities like I had. What could be more awesome? I was beyond the popular group, because we were so popular the humans couldn't even comprehend us.

"I'd always loved him. Luc," she said. I felt the blood drain from my face; this wasn't going to end well. "But they were falling all over themselves over you! *You!*" I

~ ☾ ~

pushed toward the passenger door away from her, my hand fumbling for the door handle. "And what were you but this nobody of a human who showed up wearing the same hat as me? You with your flawed appearance, powerless, helpless. But Mo and Luc were at each other's throats over you.

"It was disgusting and embarrassing. Here you were all weepy and runny and gross all the time. I didn't understand it. And now it really doesn't matter. Mo fell for you, *really* fell like became a fallen one over you, and Luc is gone because of you. We may never see him again."

I gripped the door handle, but the locks on the car snapped down.

"You. They all wanted to save you. Luc, Mo, Belle. So sickening. Why? Why you? I mean you're pretty enough, I guess, in a natural I-never-wear-make-up kind of way."

She slowed and pulled off the highway down a gravel road to the top of a hill. I finally recognized where we were. I looked ahead down the gravel road by the fence where the horses would come and snuffle at me as I cried over Julie and Mike.

"I didn't get it, what it was they were all so hot and bothered over. You are human and flawed and broken. I don't know. I guess you were in pain but still fighting. I guess they saw that in you, admired it and wanted to help you." She moved to close to me, reaching out and stroking my hair. "You're like a cornered, hunted animal. I can hear your heart beating faster. I can feel your fear."

I looked around nervously. "Are we meeting someone here?"

"Yet you don't run. Interesting." She shrugged. "They told me you'd seen an angel here once. You made divine contact. How? How did you do it?" she demanded.

~ ☾ ~

"I... I... I don't know. I didn't even know..."

"You're worse than useless. I just thought—" She stopped. No one else appeared to be coming.

"Why did you bring me here?"

"Get out of the car," she said. I had nothing left to lose except my life, and if that were to happen...

"Do it. Now," she ordered.

I shrugged, desperately confused. "Do what?"

"Make divine contact. No one on earth has been able to do that before, but they told me..."

"What, Mike? The angel?"

"Humans pretend to make contact and guardians and fallen on earth do so sometimes to make people believe or to perpetuate deception. No human has breached the veil between Heaven and Earth before without divine assistance. How did you do it?"

I looked at her blankly. She ran her fingers through her hair and started to scream. "God! God! God!" she swore, and fell in a heap on the gravel, sobbing and mumbling. "I'm sorry. I'm so sorry." Whether the apologies were directed at me or God, I couldn't tell.

I went to her. "I just... I was here upset one day...."

"Day?" She sniffed and wiped away tears.

"Errrr, no. Night. Well, evening... dusk."

She liked my response and stood, taking my hands in hers. "Dusk, that's right. That makes sense. Dusk and dawn — the borders should be thinnest. Then what?"

I pulled away, trying to make it look as though I couldn't think with her like that, but really she just creeped me out. "Then nothing. I was desperate. My dead friend appeared and spoke to me."

"You spoke back? He could hear and respond?"

"Yes. We talked for a few minutes. I thought I was going crazy. Then Luc and Mo ran up and Mike faded away, but they said they saw him too."

"Night fell. You probably only have a few minutes."

~ ☾ ~

She started nodding to herself and pacing. "What time is it?" she asked urgently.

I took out my phone and checked. My battery was dead. Dusk had hit as we had climbed out from the school. It had been night for some time now. I shrugged and showed her my phone.

"It must be close. When dawn comes, I want you to make contact. Surely that's why all the angels were drawn to you. They must have been able to sense your ability."

I shrugged again, not knowing how to respond to her. She acted crazier than normal. I'd had a long, difficult day. I'd lost my friends. I'd lost several people in the blast. I had no idea how many or who. The guardian angels had all done their job and disappeared. The others had fallen…

Then I knew. Yeah, I know, I'm slow. If she were a guardian she would have saved her soul, so she either failed, or she'd…

Violet turned to me as though she could read my mind or maybe my sudden horrified expression. "I told you where I was coming from in this," she explained. "If I wanted to hurt you or turn you over to someone else, I could have by now. I just want you to make some God-damned contact with someone who doesn't live on this God-damned giant piece of rock hell hole!"

I stayed quiet after that. I fell asleep off and on, and we waited there for hours as I shivered in the dark. Finally, as the sky started to lighten, I could see her more clearly. Darkness outlined her form, her eyes were dark, and nubs appeared on her forehead. I inhaled sharply.

"What?" she spat.

"I can see you now," was all I had to say. Her hands went to the beginnings of her horns and she hissed.

I took a step back.

~ ☾ ~

"You think this is bad? It will get worse. Much worse, if you don't talk to someone from the celestial plane right freaking now!"

I stumbled backwards at her change. The good guys had done their job and returned home. The bad guys were wreaking havoc. What about the failures? Surely there were failures out there. Couldn't one of them rescue me now to make up for their lost soul?

"*Now*! You don't have much time!" she shrieked, and grabbed me instantly. I knew I couldn't outrun her.

I walked to where I'd been when Mike had appeared, unsure what to do or if it even made a difference. "Mike?" I called feebly. "Luc?" The sky paled. I heard something in the distance, but saw the silhouettes of the horses against the yellowing sky. I rubbed my hands up and down my bare arms for warmth. I hadn't had a jacket with me when the school had blown up. "Luc? Please! I need you!" This started the tears. A bird chirped to welcome the morning.

"Something horrible has happened. Please. I am lost." I tried to sound as honest as possible, as desperate as I had when Mike had appeared. I knew I'd been through this routine several times as I'd sobbed on this gravel road and except for the single time Mike had come, my only audience was ever the horses. I understood this divine contact exercise probably wouldn't work, but Violet looked on, twisting one hand in the other with wide eyes, expecting something cataclysmic to happen.

"Oh, let me try!" she ordered, pushing past me to stand at the high point of the road. "Luc! The fallen have come. The war has begun! Get your ass back here or…" she searched for a threat, and there I stood dumbly in the impending morning. "Or Lily is toast!" She moved in a fast blur behind me and grabbed me in some kind of awkward chokehold. It was unnecessary. I knew I couldn't escape her anyway, so she didn't need to forcibly hold me, but if it got Luc to show himself, I was all for it. Go Violet!

She whipped me around to the ground and maneuvered herself with a knee at my throat and I was less amused, but still. Whatever it takes, Luc. I even started to struggle for effect.

"Come out, come out wherever you are!" she called to him. "The fallen want your girl. You have three days, and I give her to them."

The sky had lightened almost completely now. "Do you hear me Luc? Raphael? Belle? Kristabel? Time is of the essence. The war has begun. Send reinforcements or lose Earth to the fallen." Her voice trailed off with the last straggling darkness from the night.

I lay there on the gravel with her knee in my throat. "I don't think anyone is coming," I managed to croak out.

She knew it, too and stood. She held a hand down to me and helped me up.

"Who is Kristabel? Raphael?"

"Kristabel is my archangel. Raphael, the guys call him Rafe, is Luc's. And Mo's." She spoke without looking at me, barely acknowledging me.

"So what now?" I asked brushing the gravel dust from my clothes.

"Now you have three days."

~ ☾ ~

30 Three Days

I charged my phone at Violet's and called my dad to tell him I had gone to Mom's after the explosion. I told him there was too much to deal with here. Mom and Dad hadn't gotten along since the divorce, so I knew they wouldn't actually speak about it ever.

Violet's bedroom was downstairs off a small family room with a door leading outside to the backyard. Her parents had given her the run of the basement, so she hid me pretty easily. I could have tried to sneak out, but figured Mo wouldn't be looking for me here, so it was as safe as anywhere else I could run.

"I do not intend to hurt you." She kept her voice low as if she feared the angels would overhear. "You're bait. Luc will know I didn't save my soul and am still here, so odds are good I could be fallen."

"Which you are."

She sneered. "Yes, I am, but only because circumstances have dictated this, but I'm trying to redeem myself."

"By kidnapping me?"

She backhanded me hard across the face, and I realized I probably shouldn't be quite so lippy with a demon.

She rubbed the back of her hand once. "Yes, by kidnapping you to get Luc back here."

"How exactly does this redeem you?"

"This way I can help him in the war."

"What is the war?"

She gave me a disgusted look. "Read your Bible

~ ☾ ~

much? Geez. Lucifer and the fallen angels and the battle for earth? Adam and Eve? The serpent?" She paused after each one for a response from me, but I didn't feel like playing. "Is any of this ringing a bell?"

I shrugged apathetically.

"Lucifer, started the rebellion out of jealousy of the humans—"

"Why would an angel be named after the devil?" I couldn't help myself.

"Lucifer was an angel first, you moron. He just fell. After him several other very good angels have held his name. Not to mention Luke as in The Gospel of Luke. But he's not *really* named after the devil. Lucifer means 'light bearer.' It's just a bit ironic that one named Lucifer turned to the dark side."

"Maybe they had cookies." She backhanded me again, and I knew I really should learn to shut my trap.

"Lucifer was an archangel. Archangel names are often reused."

"But the human parents name the guardians who are born into their mission, don't they?" She eyed me, testing for sarcasm.

On finding none, she continued. "They do, but sometimes if the human parent is perceptive, they are able to subconsciously sense the divine connection. Or an archangel can whisper hints if it's important."

"Why would it be?"

"Why would it be for humans?" she snapped. "Names are important. They carry weight. They give an impression. They have power." She looked at me like I was an idiot again.

Our conversations were like this for the three days she held me captive. I would try to get more information about the guardians and the fallen, I would make a crack and she would inflict pain of some sort. At dawn and dusk she would drag me to the gravel road by the horses,

~ ☾ ~

and we would then re-enact the first morning we had there, trying to summon the angels to communicate. With each failure, she became more and more hostile, and at each darkening or lightening of the day, I could see her transformation more clearly.

Her horns were getting more pronounced. The darkness that seemed to outline her form became thicker. Her eyes were turning from human to cat-like. Her skin darkened by the day. Most shocking of all was the formation of the wings and the tail.

Thankfully I could only see these things at daybreak and nightfall, and they weren't visible to other humans, because it was frightening to behold. The wings weren't the soft, plumy white Belle's and Luc's had been. They were more like tightly pulled skin wings of a bat's, and the tail, long, scaly with a point at the end like a scorpion's.

How I could see this and no one else could I had no clue. Once Violet went upstairs to get me something to eat at twilight. I'm sure one of her family members would have commented on the wings and horns had they noticed. It also was apparent the otherworldly appendages weren't there physically. Well, that's not entirely true. I could feel them at daybreak and nightfall, but the wings didn't manifest physically, hinder movement or cause problems with things like sitting comfortably in a car at other times.

Where Luc and Belle had transformed immediately once their souls had been saved, Violet shifted gradually. I didn't know why, but maybe falling was more of a process than saving? Maybe if given time, a demon could turn back and repent, which is what she claimed she wanted to do.

Her plans, she maintained during my stay, were to help Luc in the war. The fallen wanted to take the earth from God. Since He was nowhere to be seen, the time was ripe.

~ ☾ ~

"How can this happen? When the fallen weren't fallen a couple of days ago?" I asked, cringing at the possible backhand, which no longer came only at sarcastic quips.

She sneered and rolled her eyes thinking me stupid. I preferred it to the backhands. "They were fallen. They just didn't know it. The call of darkness was still underneath their shiny guardian surface. They felt the call but didn't understand it. Or…"

"Or what?"

"Or there were others here we weren't aware of. Could it be?" She paced across her floor. "Could a fallen or group of fallen have already been around and planted the bomb? Could they have already corrupted souls?"

"You keep referring to the fallen as 'they,'" I observed.

"This is temporary. I will return."

"Can you?" I asked. Violet didn't make eye contact and pretended not to hear the question.

Violet had a younger brother around Owen's age. He wandered in on the second day, but Violet played it off like I was over to study. He just came in to claim something of his from the family room and was perfectly happy to avoid us. Her parents had little to nothing to do with her. They were becoming touched and though they weren't aware of why, they seemed to instinctively keep away from her.

I watched her a lot as the hours ticked by. I guessed angels or demons didn't need to be entertained constantly like humans. She didn't watch TV or listen to music or play video games. She could sit on her bed for hours, just sitting. She didn't need to eat or do anything humans did, so I had to ask for food or a drink when I got hungry or thirsty. She'd get it for me, but otherwise, she spent her time sitting, eyes narrowed, brow strained, hands rubbing against each other or a foot constantly tapping. She was anxious and running out of time.

My phone had run out of charge again and she didn't

Speak of the Devil

want me to charge it in case I tried to call the police, so no one called me. I never did listen to the messages on it from Mo or Luc. I wanted to save Luc's forever, so I could hear his voice when I needed to, but I wanted to wait until the danger with Mo was past.

We heard things from her family's conversations upstairs about the fallout from the explosion. 137 dead. The names hadn't been released yet. Since I was new to the school, I probably didn't know many. Still it was a disturbing number.

That's actually not true. I knew a few. Luc and Belle would be counted in that number. Luc and Belle would be considered dead. My chest tightened as I forced myself not to cry.

We also heard that after the explosion, riots and looting erupted in the area, and police were having a hard time controlling it. In the aftermath so far another four people had been killed, cars set aflame, stores broken into. We knew the cause.

When the family had the news on upstairs, the volume kept too loud, we heard about the continuing riots.

"The war has started." She said this as much to herself as to me. "The fallen are taking souls, twisting them. They're increasing their numbers, preparing for war."

"So who set the bomb?" I asked finally.

She glared at me. "I don't know."

"You and the others were sent here to save souls in that school. Someone upstairs knew about it in advance."

"It doesn't work like that!" She acted like I was stupid for not understanding the way Heaven worked. "No one *upstairs*," she said, mocking, "knew specifics. They just knew something would threaten souls on earth at this place and this time."

~ ☾ ~

"Spidey sense," I supplied. As usual, she was unamused. I continued. "Souls are threatened on earth all the time. What was so important about the fourteen souls they were sent to protect?"

"I don't know." She sobered. "All I know is they tend to be… special."

"Special?"

"Maybe they're going to become saints in the future, maybe they have special abilities, maybe they are going to save someone else later. They like to save heroes. It preserves divine manpower from being sent down here. But specifically, I don't know."

So I gleaned some souls are more "special" or more important than others. So my BFF was just ordinary? Unimportant? Or she was taken to "be with God" as so many at her funeral had justified. I clenched my teeth. I hated the thought of it, like I was somehow special and Julie wasn't? I really resented that. It sounded like horse crap to me.

"There must have been a demon already here. Someone we missed," she finally revealed. "A demon must have persuaded a weak, vulnerable soul to set the bomb. A soul in pain. A lost soul."

"Maybe that's why I had an angel. To keep me from being the weak soul that was corrupted."

That, she explained to me, was how the demons worked. Guardians saved souls while the fallen, demons, corrupted them. It was all very black and white. No gray areas. Except for Violet, who so desperately wanted to regain her guardianhood, or herself, as she called it. When not sleeping, I watched her sitting, grinding her teeth, stressing at the thought of losing herself completely to the demon.

On the third day, or night rather, her threatened deadline to turn me over to the demons, he came. She paraded me out in the same clothes I'd been wearing for days up to the high point of the gravel road and poked me in the back. "Do it. Last chance" She twitched her head around, on guard.

The early November breeze blew right through my flimsy t-shirt. My skin prickled and I rubbed my hands up and down my arms for warmth.

The night fell and I could see her demon form. The changes seemed complete, but all I had to compare them to were movie or TV demons. She walked with a slight hunch at the weight of the wings maybe. It wasn't really walking anymore; her movement had changed almost to a jumping or hopping gait. She sort of reminded me of the flying monkeys in *The Wizard of Oz*. Of course, I could see her wings and tail. I wondered what it looked like to the oblivious.

"Go," she ordered.

"Luc?" I called, and an immediate flash of light nearly blinded me

"I'm here." He appeared instantly and took me in his arms, his warmth jolting through me. My eyes met his and I melted, lost in them. He leaned down and kissed me softly, making me forget completely about the cold.

"I thought I'd lost you," I started gushing. "How did you come back?"

Before he could answer, Violet interrupted. "That's enough. I didn't bring him back here for *you*!"

"*You* didn't bring me back here at all. *She* did."

He was glorious and amazing. More so than I remembered, and he seemed older somehow. Wiser maybe? There was something in his eyes, a knowing or understanding. His hair was clipped neatly and his dress so different than it had been when I first saw him as a regular, human guy at school. Tonight he was dressed for war. No longer did he wear the tattered army flak jacket, but a tight black t-shirt and camouflage pants in its place. He also wore tall, black combat boots, and

~ ☾ ~

carried weapons. There was a knife strapped to his thigh, a gun in a holster at his hip, and a sword strapped to his back. He was a very real version of what he'd dressed as for Halloween.

"I want to help you fight them," she said.

"Let's get her to safety first." We turned toward her car, her loping ahead of us when I sensed their presence.

Then the same sensation I'd felt in the pizza parlor bathroom when Violet had come up behind me, hit me. The air adopted a cold, dry static feel, and a shiver ran down my spine. Before I turned to see, I heard the sound of someone slowly clapping, and Mo spoke.

"Bravo, Violet. Well done." Mo and the others made their way up the road from the other side of the hill. Sean and Hillary grinned, and loped along as Violet did, and before the darkness fell completely I could see their bat wings and demon tails, too.

I gasped.

"No, I—" she started to protest, and then looked urgently at Luc. "I'm with you. I'm on your side! I didn't tell them."

Luc held up a hand to stop her and released me from his warm embrace.

"No, she didn't actually," Mo agreed. "She'll pay for it when the time comes."

In a blur, Sean and Hillary were on opposite sides of Luc and me.

"You clean up good," Mo continued to Luc. "Any news from upstairs? Oh wait, never mind. We don't care anymore." He and the others laughed, and I saw coming over the dark peak of the road several others who echoed his sinister laughing.

"Stand down and you can be redeemed," Luc said, sending Violet into a hysterical hopping.

"Yes! Yessssss!" she cried.

"That's cute, really," Mo said, casually gesturing at

~ ☾ ~

the other demons, "But you seem to be outnumbered here."

"Leave Lily alone. She's done nothing—" he started.

"True, she's done nothing. Nothing but cry and snivel. So sure, we'll leave her alone," Mo said.

I didn't have time to take offense, and I should have felt relieved, but somehow I knew there was a catch. Even Luc paused a few seconds before asking, "She can go?"

"Sure, send her off. Violet, give her your keys." Mo talked to us so casually, like we were just getting ready to go home after school or some other ordinary daily event. Violet tossed me the keys to her car, happy to be rid of me, I'm sure, and I started for the driver's side door.

"And Luc, why don't you come with us." Hillary and Sean clamped their clawed hands onto Luc's arms as he attempted to draw the sword from his back.

"What are you doing?" Luc asked him.

"Initially we wanted Lily. I wanted to make her pay, but then I started thinking big picture." More demons streamed over the hills, all of them heading straight for Luc. "Then we saw what Violet was up to, we thought we'd intercept you. We want a hostage before the other guardians and archangels and whoever come down to fight. If they ever come down." Mo arched an eyebrow at Luc for some sort of confirmation or denial. "Anyone else coming?" Luc stood stone faced.

"Fine. We have an angel as hostage, and if the other goody goodies don't come, we'll have our first sacrifice." Mo sneered and the demons surrounding Luc started to laugh.

"No!" I shouted, dropping the keys and running toward Luc. I felt the grip of multiple clawed hands before I'd moved three feet.

"Wait!" Violet protested.

~ ☾ ~

"Take her, too, the traitor," Mo ordered, and more demons latched on to Violet.

In the short time everything went down, I saw there had to be close to forty demons, but I only recognized Mo, Sean and Hillary. Some of the others had changed to demon form, but others looked just like regular people, most of them close to my age. Briefly I thought I recognized a few from the school.

Luc struggled against his captors, but couldn't break their grip. He was outnumbered, Violet had been subdued, and they easily kept me away.

"I can't lose you again, not when I just got you back," I said softly.

"You're okay, Lily. That's all that matters to me. All that ever mattered." He stopped struggling, and they jerked him away up the road, over the hill, Violet screeching as they dragged her with them. The ones who'd been holding me slowly let me go, not even caring I was now free to fight for him or rescue him. I was nothing to them. Evil Barbie Hillary turned back with a smirk, and the demon minions walked up the road behind them, leaving me standing in the dark by the horse pasture, dazed.

~ ☾ ~

31 Down To Me

The Lily scenario: me left on my own again, helpless, lost, with no friends. The bigger picture: all of the other angels I knew were gone, and the demons were taking over my world and starting a war. My only hope, the rest of the world's only hope, was for me to save Luc. I swallowed hard past the lump in my throat, took a deep breath and did something I hadn't for some time... I prayed.

I'd been in denial since the accident. Denying God, denying He cared, but still angry at Him for taking my friends and leaving me behind. But the more I thought about it and the more I was around Luc and the other guardians, I knew. I could feel it on them. I'd died in the accident and had been near if not actually in Heaven, and I could still feel it. The warmth I felt in the presence of the guardians. I'd felt it before when I'd died. I knew the truth. So why not pray? God may have gone silent, but that didn't mean He wasn't still listening or acting. At this point, what did I have to lose?

So I reached out, stilled my mind, and prayed, not really even sure how to go about it. "Dear God, I know I've said a lot of bad things about You lately, but please forgive me. I need You, more than ever. I've needed You a lot since the accident. Please. I'm in danger. Your angels, Luc and maybe Violet if she's able to go back to being an angel... I'm rambling. They need You. Fallen angels are taking over, so if they aren't stopped... the world needs You now."

I paused as though He'd answer me, but knew it

~ ☾ ~

didn't actually work that way. Then I waited for some sort of sign, as my mind raced on for a plan.

I believed there was hope. Luc walked in my world again, so I couldn't waste time despairing, and I didn't have the luxury to just give up. I assessed the situation. They obviously didn't view me as a threat, since all I'd ever done in front of Mo was cry or shuffle through day to day like a zombie. I'd been lying around Violet's basement for three days, barely eating or sleeping, but despite that a surge of energy rushed over me, and I knew I needed to snap out of it and kick some demon ass.

If I followed in Violet's car, they'd notice. I scanned the area. It had been years since I'd ridden the neighbors' horses, but I'd spent enough time near these pastures of late, I felt they might still be familiar with me. I ripped up a handful of grass and went to the barbed wire fence, clicking my tongue and making kissing sounds. Before long, two of them had approached me and began gently nibbling the grass out of my hand.

"That's it… Dancer…? errrr… Prancer…? Damn." I couldn't remember their names and was pretty sure I was using reindeer names. "Pixie!" It came to me, as the smaller of the two looked up at me. I rubbed her velvety nose and stroked her long, white speckled neck. The larger horse wandered off, disinterested when the easy grass was gone, but Pixie liked the pets. "Remember me? I need your help," I coaxed as I slowly climbed through the barbed fence and stood next to her.

In a less than graceful manner, I managed to fling myself onto her back and pull one leg up and over. "There. I have my loyal steed, let's go Xena Warrior Princess on these demons."

I thought I saw a flash of light, and for the length of time it would take to snap a picture, Pixie appeared to

~ ☾ ~

me as a shining, white, silver-armored light war mount. In an instant, the image faded, and Pixie was just the little white horse I'd known for years.

I paused, wondering if lack of sleep, food, and bathing could cause hallucinations and dismissed what I'd seen as my imagination.

"Okay, uhhhh, now, I haven't ridden bareback before, but how hard could it be?" I asked aloud.

Pixie answered by jolting off up the hill in the direction of the bad guys while I gripped handfuls of mane and clamped onto her body with my legs wondering how I'd get her to stop.

Angels and demons could move at super speed if they wanted to, and once Pixie and I cleared the hill I could see they were moving quickly but not impossibly quickly. Mo probably wanted to taunt Luc and savor this as long as possible. I pulled back on Pixie's mane. "Whoa girl. I want to catch up to them but not be obvious about it."

Surprisingly, she responded as though she understood. She slowed to a bouncy trot continuing in the direction they had gone. I kept them in sight as long as I could. I knew I had to follow to see where they ended up, but I could go only go so far on my horse before a fence would stop us.

Again, as though responding to my thoughts, Pixie's paced quickened. She veered and jumped the barbed wire fence, landing on the gravel road to its left. She proceeded calmly, following at a safe distance behind the demon gang.

My heart pounded from the jump, and I felt as if everywhere I could sweat did and all at once. "Okay, that works."

We followed, unnoticed, about the length of a football field behind them for a few hours before they veered off into another pasture. I pulled back on Pixie's mane and

~ ☾ ~

watched. The demons gathered around a copse of trees off the road. Within a few minutes, a bonfire roared up lighting the area around them.

   Small trees and shrubs lined the gravel road, so in the shadows I could easily keep from being seen, but once the sun came up, hiding would be more difficult. I nudged the horse closer at a slow pace.

   I'd been a prisoner at Violet's house for three days, and while she'd fed me when asked, it had been several hours since I'd eaten. I hadn't been allowed to go upstairs to take a shower, and she didn't care that I'd been in the same clothes the whole time, either. Frankly, I'd been too worried about the explosion, the riots, and whether or not Violet was going to hand me over to Mo and the other demons to worry about my clothes. But now as I spied on them from afar, I wished I was better equipped.

   I wish my phone was charged so I could use my GPS to see where exactly I am. I wish I was dressed for hiking gravel roads and traipsing through fields. I wish my clothes were at least dark. I wish I had a silver cross necklace, food, water, weapons.... Anything, I thought to myself. It didn't change the reality of the situation. I had myself and a horse named Pixie, who was okay just to nibble on the grass edging the road.

   The demons were still a distance away. No one had ever mentioned to me whether or not they had great eye sight or anything. I hoped staying behind the brush along the road in the dark while they were in the fields looking at a bonfire gave me cover enough to keep me from being seen. I watched them, but none glanced in my direction. We were far from the highway and no city lights could be seen glowing on the horizon, so I assumed we were out in the boonies. They didn't seem to be too concerned about being spotted or followed. That worked to my advantage.

   I slowly dismounted and gave Pixie a long stroke

~ ☾ ~

down her neck and back and patted her a few times. She stayed, neck bowed, munching on the tall grass along the road. I took a deep breath and tried to get closer.

I crept along the road trying to stay behind the large pine trees or bigger shrubs to remain unnoticed, to see if I could find anything out. I counted over forty demons in the field. They were setting up a make shift camp around the bonfire. Luc and Violet were chained back to back against a tree off to the side. Every now and then I could hear her screech, but Luc remained still and quiet. Had he given up?

I needed to find out what they were planning, but right now Luc looked as safe as someone could be in the midst of a gang of demons. At least they weren't hurting him. They seemed to be... well, acting like teenagers having a field party, but with hostages. Some of the demons were drinking, some were making out. They were all laughing and talking. Just hanging out basically. It reminded me vaguely of parties I'd gone to when I lived with my mom, parties where I faked it and carried a drink around all night.

I could try to fake my way into the demons and find out their plan. No, they could probably see all the time what I could only see at sunrise and sunset — their demon forms. I had to find a way to get close so I could hear their plans. I needed to know how much time Luc had before they killed him or converted him. He and Violet were still chained up, so at least Luc was still a guardian, and Violet was still fighting her demonhood.

Suddenly behind me I heard a strange sound, something like water splashing. I looked back to see Pixie off the road on the opposite side of the field, drinking from a stream. I turned back to the demons, thinking nothing of it at first. Then I decided, I could at least wash my hands and face and maybe take a drink if the stream wasn't too gross.

~ ☾ ~

Since the little creek ran on the other side of the road and dipped down in the opposite pasture, I stayed completely hidden from any demons who might be scouting, though it didn't look like they were bothering. I washed my hands and splashed some water on my face while I gathered my thoughts. I noticed the stream ran under the road through a culvert. Curiously I moved toward it and looked through. I could see through the pipe to the other side of the road, into the field where the demons were partying. The stream continued straight through the field, not far from where Mo and the others had amassed, and it had cut a winding path across the ground, like a little ditch that ran past them with tall grass and reeds along the edges where the farmers couldn't mow easily. I hadn't seen the little trench because it had been so dark, but now I knew I could use it to spy on the fallen angels.

Pixie looked up at me, water dripping from her snout and she nickered quietly, while I headed over the road. The demons were a good 100 feet or so off the road in the field, and the dark of night kept me hidden, as far as I could tell. The orange glow of the bonfire drew most eyes. I slipped through the barbed wire fence, snagging my t-shirt, and slid down about three feet to the creek bed on the demon side of the road. I crawled on my belly in the direction of the bonfire, staying on the bank of the creek closer to the demons in hopes that gave me the best cover from anyone glancing my way.

I crawled slowly, trying not to disturb the reeds. Here I was again, sneaking up on Luc and the others to spy. It reminded me of crawling across the wooden planks high about the theater stage, so I could eavesdrop on the guardians just days ago. If only we could go back, before Mo had turned, before the explosion. I wondered if there was something I could've done. If I'd stayed with Mo, would he have still fallen?

~ ☾ ~

Speak of the Devil

My life had been so simple before the accident. The only worries I had were to dread math class or worry about being a nerd at school until the accident came and changed everything. I'd tried to run away, tried to adjust here. Things could've gotten to be normal here, but no, I had to fall in with a bunch of angels. Now the school was closed since half of it had been blown apart, Kansas City had been overcome with riots, and demons were threatening to convert everyone and kill those who resisted in order to take over the world. Those recruited would be called to fight the angels who came to protect us, and the war would ensue.

Probably the largest demon gang going had captured Luc, the only guardian I knew of on Earth. The other guardians had gone back home or were in hiding, maybe ashamed for failing their task, maybe afraid to face the fallen onslaught. So basically the battle between good and evil, the war of the demons and angels, and maybe even the world's existence was down to me, a teenage girl who hated math, read comic books and fantasy novels, watched science fiction on TV, needed a shower in a serious way, and had no weapons or powers or abilities....

My head started to throb as I thought it all through. *We're screwed.*

~ ☾ ~

32 Last Ditch Effort

I took a final deep breath before moving in as close as I could get without leaving the trench and being spotted. Slowly I approached one end of the circle of the fallen and paused to listen, perched on the small bank of the creek in the mud, no longer worried my white shirt would attract attention and trying to ignore the fact that I was freezing to death out here in the dead of night with only this flimsy t-shirt on. My white shirt, now black with filth after crawling through fifty feet of sticky mud, camouflaged me fine now.

After a few minutes of listening to demons party, I could pick out Mo in the distance. On the opposite side of the fire, of course, so I'd be unable to hear any of what he said on the matter. "Dammit," I swore under my breath, wondering if I could draw him this way, even though I realized how stupid that would be.

A scuffle broke out, and I could hear the sounds of feet shuffling and people falling and rolling on the ground.

"Yeah!" someone cheered and others followed with some hoots and hollers and some grunts sprinkled in. A fight?

"Hey!" Mo shouted from across the way. "Sean!"

Ah, Sean was at it again, starting a fight with some other demon. Typical.

"Break it up!" one of the other demons snarled and the noises subsided.

A large flump noise came along with a strong exhale of breath near my hiding spot. "Are you okay?" a female

~ ☾ ~

fallen asked. I slowly peeked out through the reeds to make sure she wasn't talking to me. Outlined by the glow of the bonfire I saw Sean sitting on the ground only ten feet or so away, and a girl I didn't know knelt next to him.

"This?" Sean chuckled and wiped the side of his mouth with the back of his hand. "This ain't nothing.'"

She snuggled in next to him, and he put his arm around her. I think I'd seen her in class before, but didn't know her name.

"Do you want something to drink?" she asked him.

"Nah, I'm good. We should be ready and alert anyway. All these idiots drinkin' are just going to miss all the fun."

Please ask him what's going to happen. Please ask him what's going to happen. Please ask him what's going to happen, I thought, wishing I could magically control what she said.

"Are they really going to kill them?" she asked, as though she'd heard my plea.

"Convert or kill the halo, those are the orders." He smeared the blood from the corner of his mouth on the shoulder of the sleeve of his black Judas Priest t-shirt.

"What is Mo waiting for?" she asked in a small, inquisitive voice.

Sean turned on her. "What is *Mo* waiting for?"

She pulled back from him.

"What do you mean what is Mo waiting for? Mo isn't in charge here!"

"Oh, I thought—" Her eyes darted toward Mo, who stood close to Barbie girl, talking.

"What are *we* waiting for, is what you meant to say!" His voice raised, blood boiling as usual, clearly having heard the call of wrath.

"Yes," she submitted. "When are you going to—?"

His anger washed away as quickly as it had flared,

~ ☾ ~

and he stared at his former friend chained near the fire. He took another deep breath. "Mo wants them to be able to see." That he immediately deferred to Mo wasn't lost on me. It was on the girl, though. Super smarts isn't one of a demon's powers apparently.

"Who?"

"What, are you stupid? The guardians back home! Mo wants them to feel the death." Sean pushed himself painfully up and stormed away, leaving the girl to sit alone. She soon got bored and chose to head over next to the hangers-on around Mo.

He wants the guardians to see? He wants the angels in Heaven to witness Luc's conversion or execution? Reflexively I pulled out my phone to see how much time I had until dawn, but the blank screen of a phone that hadn't been charged in days gave me no answer.

I wanted to heave the phone into the field, like bad guys always did with their guns in movies as soon as they ran out of ammo, as if the gun were useless forever once that happened, but I shoved it into my back pocket instead. My kingdom for a charged cell phone.

Luc was farther down past the bonfire, so I crawled along the creek bed some more to get closer to him and Violet. There were fewer fallen ones around them, almost like they were repulsed or frightened that being near Luc might hurt them in some way.

Violet screeched and pleaded, but the others ignored her. As I got closer, I could see she strained so hard against her bonds that blood smeared her wrists, while Luc remained still.

They'd taken his weapons from him, and I saw the sword, gun and dagger lying near the fire. The gun and the knife looked like standard military issue weapons, but the sword... There was something about it. It didn't just shine and reflect the light from the fire, it seemed to glow a slivery white from within. I'd doubted God before meeting these people, but I believed with everything I had that the sword was magic or divine... a holy weapon to defeat the demons. Even a mere mortal like me could see it.

If I could get to the sword, cut the chain from Luc's wrists and free him...

"Well, well, welly, well." Mo's voice came from behind me, the female fallen I'd seen by Sean's side earlier stood by him. "Have you ever heard the saying, 'Curiosity killed the cat'?"

I stood, seeing how the jig was up. Luc looked at me, eyes wide. He tried to break free from his chains now.

"You, darlin', are the cat," Mo explained. "Tie her up," he ordered, and the clawed hands were on me. "On second thought, I have a better idea. This party was getting rather boring, don't you think?" Fallen angels cheered. Some held their beers up triumphantly while others downed what they were drinking before throwing the empties in the field. "The demon traitor was going to be our pre-show, but now maybe Lily can be our show opener."

"No!" Luc strained against his chains.

"Oh yes." Mo moved in close to me and brushed my cheek with the back of his hand, almost gently. I turned my head away, and he grabbed me by the hair, jerking my head back. Slowly he moved in, licking me from my collar bone up to my temple. I squeezed my eyes tightly, willing myself somewhere else.

He laughed cruelly. "I've been wanting to know what it would be like to have you," he said quietly, just for me to hear. "You teased me before, acted like you were interested, and I fell for you." He brushed a tear trickling from the corner of my eye away with his thumb, holding my hair so I couldn't turn away.

"I thought I loved you. But that was then, and things have changed. I was going to let you go for old time's sake, but you just can't leave well enough alone, can you? Always spying and listening in. So," he said louder, "now I'll find out what it is to have you. Possess you. In more ways than one." He sneered at me. Any love that had been there now gone. "And your boy toy here can watch!"

"I'll kill you!" Luc shouted. "All of you! Every. Last. One!"

My eyes lingered longingly on the sword by the fire. I'd been so close, only to be dragged away by my hair. Luc had been calm and had accepted his fate, but with me in Mo's hands, Luc struggled and bucked against his ties, his angel stoicism gone. I'd only made things worse.

Mo, still gripping a handful of my hair, pulled me closer to the fire while his demon hordes parted to let him through. He threw me down to the ground, grinning. I'm sure on any normal day, the roughness of his actions would have been painful, but lucky for me, I was an expert at zombie mode. Luc's calm strength may have left him for now, but mine held firm.

"What, no crying?" he asked. I looked at him blankly. "We couldn't shut you up before with all of your whining and moaning. Now nothing?"

I shrugged. "Like you said, things have changed."

"Fair enough." He walked casually towards me before he struck me across the face.

A short laugh escaped my lips. Backhands must be a demon thing. Luckily Violet had prepped me for this. It hardly fazed me.

"Find something funny?" he asked.

"I used to find you funny."

"If you're trying to find goody-goody angel Mo in here somewhere, it doesn't work that way, sweetie. You've watched too many movies."

Damn. It had been worth a try. He reached down and grabbed me by the front of my shirt, pulling me up to

~ ☾ ~

Speak of the Devil

stand, and jerked me over next to Luc, but I noticed Mo kept a wide berth from the angel who struggled to break free.

Then Mo kissed me, hard and brutal, but I stood there like a statue. He would get no pleasure from my resistance. I didn't care anymore. My world was crumbling around me, on a larger scale than it had when I'd lost Mike and Julie. I survived death. I'd survived losing my friends. I survived the explosion, the loss of Luc, the riots, even the realization a war of epic proportions loomed. I may not be Super Girl, but if nothing else, I was a survivor.

Unlike our first kiss, full of tenderness and sweetness, this kiss was vicious and cruel. That didn't matter to me now. I pushed the kiss away. I pushed what it meant once and what it meant now away. I gave it no more importance than any other mundane physical exercise. A cough. A sneeze. A hiccup. It was nothing to me.

Mo pulled back with a smile until he saw the deadness in my gaze. His eyes narrowed and he shoved me back to the ground. I responded as though someone had just brushed past me at the mall. It didn't matter. I tuned the cheers from the demons out with ease, but Luc shouted. Almost howling like a wounded animal. That I couldn't turn off. I clung to apathy mode, and tried to quiet it.

Mo didn't respond to his fallen gang or to Luc either. He focused on me and getting a response, making me all the more determined to remain calm. He leapt on top of me, pushing my back down against the ground. I gave him nothing. He kissed me again. Nothing. He slapped me. As my head was thrown to the side from the hit, I saw I was almost within reach of the sword by the fire. I turned my head back to face him on top of me, clouding over that piece of information, so he wouldn't see the hope in my eyes.

~ ☾ ~

He took hold of my shirt at the V-neck, and ripped it in half down the middle. I tried not to react, but now my shirt lay open in front of dozens of demons. This was definitely out of my comfort zone. My breath froze in my chest, and I felt my heart racing and the cold, dry static crackling around him; this wasn't the Mo I'd known. I had no idea what he was capable of anymore. I could act strong if I had to, but inside I screamed. If it were just me, I could handle it. I could go out of myself, leave my body, and take my mind elsewhere if what I imagined was coming next actually happened, but I couldn't take it with Luc there having to watch. I could deal with my suffering, but Luc's pain and feeling of helplessness and failure… I couldn't handle that.

Mo grinned, sensing my concern. Then the flood of shouts from the others broke through the wall of indifference I tried to keep up, and Luc's fear was plastered on his face. I took a deep breath trying to regain control. For him.

Mo pushed my legs apart with a knee and reached for my belt. This had gotten bad, fast. What did I expect from demons? I looked frantically now toward the sword, tipping my hand, but it bought me another few seconds of reprieve, while Mo stopped to reach over and grab it.

"This? Did you want this?" He mocked as he held it above me. "You don't even know what this is."

My heart pounded, but I tried to remain calm.

"This, honey, is the Spirit Sword and you're right to have wanted it. This isn't good for demons. But it's not good for humans either." He put the blade up to my throat. "Nor is it good for halos." He pulled it from my neck to point at Luc, who quieted for now, waiting. "A sharp edge is a sharp edge. But this sword has been touched by the Holy Spirit, so it has power to bring light and goodness and all that crap." He threw it aside like

Speak of the Devil

another empty beer can, but with his demon strength, it had gone far out of my reach or Luc's. "Maybe we can play with it later, you and me." He grinned his demon grin at me, and bent down kissing me.

So far I'd been able to block this out, but he got to me. I tried to pull away, but he grabbed my face and held me in place, his tongue violently finding its way in my mouth. His hands slid down the sides of my body and started working at my belt again.

"Mo! You won't come back from this!" Luc warned.

"I never want to come back from this," Mo answered, his intentions to defile me evident in his tone.

I tried to fight him off and could see Luc raging and trying to escape, neither of us could do anything to stop it. Mo got my belt unbuckled and yanked it from the loops on my jeans tossing it into the crowd of demons. Then he leaned in, smothering me with a painful kiss. Once he'd kissed me with such tenderness and love, but this was all violence and hate.

"I convert!" Violet blurted out. "I accept my demonhood. I want to join your group!"

Mo pulled his face off of mine, and I gasped for air. He exhaled an exasperated sigh which smelled of beer. "What?"

"I convert. I don't want to be killed with him," she gestured to Luc. "I accept what I am."

"Mo, it's a trick," Hillary said. "She's buying time."

"No! It's true!" Violet shrieked.

"We'll deal with her later. I'm busy," and he climbed on me again, mouth smashing onto mine, tongue violating my mouth, while his hands ran from my neck, over my chest, down my stomach, to the ridge of my jeans.

"There's no time left!" Violet insisted. "The veil is thinning even now! I pledge my loyalty to the fallen cause!"

~ ☾ ~

Mo pulled away again, and I got my hand up to wipe across my mouth. He looked to the skies. "Hill?"

Hillary glanced upward as well. "It's close. I'm starting to feel a chill."

"Let me help!" Violet went on. "I want to help kill the angel! Let me help!"

Mo pulled himself off of me. "I'll finish with you later, after your boyfriend is dead. Or maybe he'll convert, and we'll both have some of you."

I shuddered at the thought. "Not in a million years would Luc do something like that." Grateful for the reprieve, I wiped my mouth on my shoulder,

"I'm not stupid," Mo said to Violet. "I don't trust you. I don't know what your game is, but I'm not unchaining you. After Luc is slain — not before — you'll go free."

Violet screeched and hopped in her bindings.

"We should prepare." Hillary glanced toward me. "We've wasted enough time."

"If I want your opinion I'll give it to you," Mo snapped. He adjusted himself in his jeans then made a rally motion. "Set up the circle you fools. What are you waiting for?" A handful of the demons busily went to making some sort of ritual circle in the field.

Violet's head down, her eyes searched frantically for something. Luc, too, had calmed as he glanced my way. "I'm sorry," he said quietly. "All I ever wanted to do was protect you. Since the very first day..."

They'd left me untied again, knowing how useless I was. I searched for the sword. Hillary stood with it in her hand, point in the earth. "Ah ah ah!" She wagged a finger at me. Yup I was useless.

"I have something for you, in my side pocket." Luc glanced down at the pocket of his camos on the side of his thigh. "I got it for you a while ago, at the Renaissance Festival."

I glanced around before reaching in and finding a

~ ☾ ~

small velvet ring box. I frowned.

"It's all I can give you now," he said.

I opened the box to find the beautiful silver Claddagh ring I'd eyed at the festival, remembering he'd been there with Violet and must have seen me looking at it.

"There's a cross in the design, where the hands grasp the heart. It can protect you. Silver and crosses can help against demons," he started to explain.

"I know, Violet told me." Tears stung my eyes. I put the ring on. "Thank you." I put my arms around him and kissed him, a kiss full of love and power and purity. If he weren't chained, it would have been perfect. But there was no way I could free him. Fallen angels were everywhere. "I've got to get you out of here."

Violet's head suddenly snapped up. "You will," she said, low and urgent.

Warily I turned to her. "What do you mean?" I didn't know which team she was on anymore.

"Remember the plan," she said.

"What?" I didn't get it. The female fallen who'd tried to chat up Sean moved in closer with a few friends, watching us.

"I don't know what to do," I admitted. "Luc, I love you and when you left, I didn't know how to manage."

"But you did."

"If they kill you..."

"You'll be fine, Lily. Look at me. You may not realize it, but you are strong. You've been through more than most people could cope with and have come out smarter and stronger. You're a fighter."

I scoffed at him.

"Maybe not a throwing punches kind of girl, but you felt the pain from the loss of your friends. You didn't numb it like the others. You experienced all of the emotions that came with your grief. You cried, you raged, you defied it until you could accept it. A weaker

~ ☾ ~

person would have numbed it away and ignored it.

"I wanted to help you from the first day I saw you, as did Mo and Belle and probably even some of the juniors, but the truth was, you didn't need saving. We did. We were drawn to you because we needed you, not the other way around. All of us have been touched by you."

"I don't know what you mean." I wiped the tears away.

"Your pain came from the loss of your friends. Your pain came from love. That was something we hadn't truly known or understood here on earth. We were here to work, for a job, and the only love we'd known was a divine one... His love and our love for Him. Yours was... real and earthly. Not selfish, not self-serving, not one of duty; one which sprang up within you and bloomed around you."

I shook my head, still not getting it.

"We were here to save people like you, but you, with your example, saved us," he smiled, tears glistening in his eyes. Violet sniffed. "That could have been me," he tilted his head towards some demons gathered by the fire. "Or Belle..."

"Look, Loverboy," Violet's voice cracked. "There's no more time. I've been coming here for the last three days and watching for the exact times for twilight and dawn." She gave me a pointed look. "I can feel it now, and there's no more time for this. Lily?"

My mind clouded with everything he'd just said and the sounds of the demons behind me. She tried to tell me something, but I didn't even know whether I trusted her or not. I heard Mo in the background barking orders at the demons.

Luc's face seemed to brighten. "Yes! Lily. You got this!"

Why did he keep saying that to me? *I got nothin'*, I thought. I was just a regular girl, cold and hungry,

~ ☾ ~

wearing a dirty ripped shirt. I'd already died once, with nothing special about me except the love stuff he'd just mentioned and the ability to talk to angels in Heaven...

Finally I clued in and looked at Luc, beautiful, shining, angel winged Luc, a slight halo glowing over his head now. That was new. And Violet, whose horns seemed to have subsided some, and her wings weren't nearly as batty as they'd been earlier...was she getting better?

"All right everyone. Gather round," Mo called for the horde to hear. His horns were long and pointed, demon tail, bat wings. I knew if I could see through his sneakers his feet would be cloven hooves. He neared us, loping since the demon form was prone to strange movement. "It's time to get started."

I could see the angel characteristics of Luc and the demon traits of the fallen. I only had a few minutes while the sun breached the horizon.

"Angels!" I called. "Guardians of Heaven!"

For a beat after I shouted, my voice raised to the skies, the demons froze in their tracks. But only for a second, before Mo yelled, "Stop her!"

"Angels above!" I cried out faster, unfortunately not as familiar with praying as I should be. "The fallen have taken over! Earth is in danger!" Demons were upon me, trying to clamp my mouth shut. I managed to jerk my head to the side, out of someone's clawed grip. "Demon War!" The hand twisted my neck back and held my mouth shut.

"What do you want us to do with her? Kill her?" The demon holding me asked Mo. His brows furrowed at this, as if the thought of me actually getting killed hadn't crossed his mind, but then his face clouded over. He was a demon now after all.

"If you have to."

The demon nodded sharply. Nothing happened and seconds ticked away. I had to try one more time. I bit down on his clawed hand, hard. He jerked it back, yelping in pain.

I raised my hand with my ring toward them. The demons on me hissed and shied away, shielding themselves from the silver symbol.

"*Mike!*" I screamed, shredding my throat to do so as loud as I possibly could.

What followed may as well have been in slow motion. The demon who'd tried to silence me clutched his bitten hand, and his head turned back to me at my scream, the other demons froze once again. Luc stood hands bound behind him still chained to a tree, eyes closed as he concentrated. Violet, chained as well, bounced up and down with excitement beside him.

Suddenly I felt the wave of warmth only a second before Mike appeared in front of me, my lost friend from back home. My friend, my angel. Brilliant and shining, with a full set of wings, a halo and silver armor. I smiled at first, so proud of him I could burst, but then realized the danger he would now be in.

He smiled back, relaxed, confident, looking very peaceful and pure. He reached out to me, but behind him I saw the hordes snap out of their stunned inertia and go for Mike. "*No!*" I shouted to warn him, but this just made him smile more.

What have I done? I wondered. I'd just given them another angel to slay, another person I cared about.

My heart was screaming and broken; then the flashes of light started. One here, one behind the circle, one behind me — a brilliant lightning storm across the field. Four, five, six, until the flashes were so many they seemed to be as one, blanketing the pasture in brilliant light.

"Halos!" a female fallen shouted an alarm. "Halos are coming!" As if they didn't know what the brilliant blasts of light were.

~ ☾ ~

Speak of the Devil

The demon shrieks came next, and as I saw the ones closing in on Mike, he drew a shiny sword, similar to the one on the ground, and with a spinning motion, dropped three demons who instantly turned to dust at their deaths. With a quick blur he was at the tree, using the blade to slice through Luc's and Violet's chains. "Don't worry." He took off in a blaze of shining metal and demon screams.

I stood there stunned. I surveyed the field. Belle looked wickedly angelic in her silver breastplate and winged helm, wielding her two short swords like a Valkyrie dancer. Luc, now free, went for Hillary and the Spirit Sword, automatically joining the fray.

Gregor appeared more energetic than I'd ever seen him. His long hair had been trimmed and he stood straight and tall, armored and winged, weapon in hand. Wow, he'd been awake long enough to save someone in the blast? My thoughts were all jumbled up against each other by the hundreds as I watched the battle unfold around me.

Cassie and Tim from the junior guardian squad were there, too. Cassie gave me a quick smile, before slashing at demons with her double bladed sword.

It was such a relief to see them back, along with hundreds of other angels I'd never seen before, turning demons to piles of ash left and right.

I stood in awe of the battle. I witnessed an actual fight of good and evil. Angels and demons warred before me, and I only had seconds left before I wouldn't be able to see them in their true forms. I watched, soaking it all in so I would never forget it.

"Horns versus Halos!" someone shouted a battle cry. Then I heard a horse whinny, and saw in the dawn Pixie winged and galloping toward the fray, rearing up and crashing down upon a demon. Pixie?

I could see movement from the corner of my eye, one

of the ruddy, bat-winged creatures heading toward me, knife drawn. In the time it took me to turn for a better look at whether he was actually rushing me or just running in battle, it was too late. He came toward me, and I had no time to run.

His mouth opened in a yell showing his pointed teeth, and he leapt at me, like a wolf taking down a rabbit, both hands reaching in my direction. My muscles tensed reflexively, about to jerk me in one direction or the other, or bring the ring up to deter him, but I knew it would be too late. I knew Luc was too far to reach me, I couldn't see the other angels I knew. This was going to be the end of me.

Someone jumped in front of me, drawing a blade in a horizontal motion, cutting the demon's throat. The attacking demon fell with a thud before me, and Mo turned to look at me. For a second, I saw the bouncy, puppy-like Mo I'd been attracted to at the beginning of the year. His eyes looked happy for a flash, and relieved. He'd just saved me, like he'd wanted to all along. Like he'd believed was his entire purpose on earth. His horns faded and his wings lightened. "Lily, I—" he began right before a sword came out through the front of his chest.

The other demons I'd seen slain turned to ash, almost as if they'd been burned in the flames of hell. But Mo stood next to me, sword impaling him, blood dripping from his mouth. He stared at me in surprise and shock, and then appeared to relax, the tension vanishing from his face. He looked peaceful before he crumpled to the ground.

Behind him stood Sean, full horns and bat wings, tail and all, holding the other end of the sword.

"What's he think he's doing? Still trying to save you?" Sean pulled the blade from his old friend, and wiped it clean on Mo's shirt, as Mo lay on the ground, gasping for breath.

~ ☽ ~

"Why did you do that?" I asked as I knelt beside Mo.

He just laughed and shook his head. "The same reason I'm going kill you. Because I feel like it!" He started to lunge over Mo's body at me, but with what little strength Mo had left, he grabbed Sean by the shirt and pushed him back.

"Not today," he said, and spit out a mouthful of blood.

Before Sean could regain his balance and come at me again, Violet bounded up behind him, dragging a blade across his throat. "Dust to dust, Seany," she said.

A brief flash of terror crossed his face, graying an instant before he turned to ashes.

The sun reached the point where I couldn't see anyone's true form anymore, and no further angels struck down. But in looking around the guardians clearly had the battle under control.

Tears streamed down my face when I saw Mo struggling to live. I felt like an idiot, but I had cared for him once. I had hurt him and he'd fallen. It wasn't so different from my friends back home turning to alcohol or drugs to numb their pain. He'd turned to his demon side, and it had been my fault.

He took my hand and tried to talk. A sincere smile spread across his face and his eyes lit up. "I saved you." He said before falling limp in my arms.

"I know." I choked on my sobs. But he didn't shimmer and disappear. He didn't turn to ashes. He simply lay there, dead in my lap.

Violet squatted down next to us over the ashes which had once been Sean. "Mo didn't turn to ash!" She beamed. "He redeemed himself. We can help him, you know. If you want to."

"Yes!"

"I don't know if *I* can anymore, but I'll try." She held her hands over him and closed her eyes. Her lips moved slightly, but I couldn't hear what she said. The battle quieted around us. Then, a greenish light outlined Mo, and Violet gasped as the power coursed through her. His wounds closed and his breathing slowly restarted in his chest.

Luc leaned over us instantly. "What's going on here?"

Mo sat up, eyeing the spot that had been a hole in his chest only minutes ago. "Violet, you did it!"

Luc jerked him up forcefully.

"Luc, he saved me."

"That's nice, but he has to answer for his crimes, for his falling. Take her," Luc said motioning to Violet. Belle seized her by the back of her neck.

"She helped me, too, and brought back Mo!" I protested.

"It's okay, Lily," Violet said.

"If she's truly fought her fall from grace, they'll know," Luc pointed upwards.

"It will be handled fairly," Mo said. "We're in good hands now."

Mike approached us, as did Cassie and Tim. All of the guardians I knew were in good shape.

"You're okay?" Mike asked me.

"I'm fine."

"Good. I'd hate to have saved you once just to have you harmed only months later."

"What?"

Mike laughed and took my hand. "The car accident."

"You were *my* angel? I was *your* soul?"

He glanced at Luc nervously. "Well, you were then anyway." He smiled at me.

"But these fallen angels... when they died they turned to ash. I saw you, your body in the coffin. I went to your funeral!"

Mike smiled. "Angels can disappear in a flash or leave a body behind."

"Demons get dusted," Luc said. "Once they've fallen

and crossed completely over, it's ashes to ashes."

"So they're demons forever?"

"Not necessarily." Mike jumped in. "There are a few ways they can be redeemed, but they are rare occurrences."

"Very rare," Luc added.

"There is such thing as grace, you know," Violet said. "It's not always just that we fall, but how far we rise after falling."

"That's what the big guy says anyway," Mike explained with a smile.

"He's a strong believer that you can't succeed without ever having failed," Luc added.

I'd figure it all out eventually, but now information overloaded my brain. Not to mention I'd just witnessed a historic and massively spiritual battle.

"I'll take these two back with me." Mike nodded toward Mo and Violet. "Lily—"

Mike became very serious and took my hands in his. "You know how when people die, everyone says, 'They wouldn't want you to be sad. They would want you to move on and be happy'?" I nodded.

"It's true. We've seen you grieve, and I know for a fact, we wished for you to move on and live your life."

I nodded again, but then what he said hit me. "We?"

He squeezed my hands. "Me and Julie. She's so proud of you right now, I can't even tell you."

"Julie? You talk to Julie?"

He didn't reveal anything else; he just smiled his bright angel smile. "Lily, take care of yourself. Remember, life goes on."

"You always say that," I said, smiling and tearing up simultaneously.

"It's always true. Keep the faith."

I jumped into his arms giving him a big hug. "Will I see you again?"

~ ☾ ~

"Anything is possible."

"Tell her—"

He held his hand up to stop me. "She knows." And with that he, Mo, and Violet were gone in a literal flash.

The angels I knew regrouped around me. "You did well," Tim said to me. "If not for your ability, we wouldn't have known what was happening here."

"I don't understand. Can't you watch us from above?" I asked sniffling and wiping away my tears.

"Not lately. Not in His absence," Tim admitted.

"No one has located… Him?"

"Not yet," Luc responded. "But once we returned home, the archangels were there to help us as much as possible."

"So what now?" I asked. The field was littered with piles of ashes and other guardians were taking away demons with their clawed hands restrained behind their backs.

The guardians looked from one to the other. Luc exhaled sharply. "Now, the guardians return home, interrogate the captured demons and report back."

Belle spoke up, "This was the first fallen formation, so now that it's been contained, all is safe. If it hadn't been—."

"Things would have spread," Cassie continued. "Others on earth would have fallen and joined up. The battle for earth would have been much greater."

"But *was* it completely contained?" Luc asked, his face darkening, while the other guardians just looked at him. "I mean, we *saw* Mo, Sean and Hillary change."

"Right," Tim answered.

"So, who planted the bomb?" he asked. Tim glanced to Kara and Cassie while Belle stepped up beside Luc.

"What are you saying?" she asked.

I pieced it together. "Fourteen angels, all at the school at the same time where a bomb was planted. Some of the angels fell *after* the explosion. Who were the fallen who set the bomb in the boiler room down by the theater in the first place?"

"I don't think our work here in Kansas City is over," Luc added. The others glanced around knowingly.

I went to Luc and took him in my arms. He didn't wear armor like the others since he'd been ambushed, so I felt the warmth of his embrace and fell into him. He brought his hand up behind me and stroked my hair.

"We'll get back and coordinate with Kristabel and Rafe," Tim told him.

Then it dawned on me, and I pulled back sharply.

"Wait! You're going now?" I started to panic.

Luc looked down at me and smiled broadly. "They are."

"Not you?"

He shook his head. "I'm staying."

"What? How?" Not that I was complaining.

"The archangels decided it wasn't safe to leave Earth unattended in His silence, and since you're the only one with the ability to open the boundaries between Heaven and Earth, you should be protected at all costs." Luc smirked his infamous smirk at me.

"You're staying with me?" I could barely speak through the huge smile spread across my face.

"It appears you need a guardian… again!" The angels laughed and their musical laughter chimed around us. They said their good-byes and as quickly as they'd come, they vanished, leaving Luc and me in the field with a dying bonfire, piles of ash, and a plain speckled horse down by the stream.

~ ☾ ~

33 Ending

I climbed under the barbed wire fence, leading Luc to Pixie who must have jumped back over it after the fight. Standing next to my brave steed I turned to Luc.

"Hmmm." He eyed me.

"Hmmm what?"

"Nothing, just you and that horse. It's sort of Joan of Arc like."

"Huh?"

"I just see flashes of silver armor and you charging in." He shook his head. "Never mind."

I gave him a funny look. Angels were weird sometimes.

Luc and I rode Pixie back to Violet's car, returning the horse to the pasture. "Animals can be divine too, you know?"

"That could explain all the help Pixie gave me in my time of crisis and in the battle."

Violet's keys were still on the ground where I'd flung them, so we headed to her place so I could clean up and borrow some clothes. Luc knew a way to get in unnoticed, so her family wouldn't be alerted. I didn't ask how he knew about it, and really didn't want to know. I cleaned up and snagged some clean, non–ripped apart clothing to go home in.

My heart pounded as we pulled in my driveway, but everything was how I'd left it, and when I entered, my dad smiled and hugged me. My gamble had worked, and he hadn't tried to reach mom for verification.

Owen and Sophie were safe. Owen was anxious to

hear what had happened since I'd left. He was no dummy. He knew I'd left with Violet and hadn't gone to my mom's, but he trusted me and hadn't alerted the parental units.

As far as the school went, they stabilized what could be salvaged and were already working on rebuilding. About half of the school had functioning classrooms, and the state brought in some temporary trailers for the rest of us to use 'till the end of the year.

Luc rarely left my side, and that was fine with me. Things were obviously empty and strange at school with so many people having been killed or injured in the explosion, turned to demons and destroyed, or gone home to Heaven. I missed Belle. We hadn't spent a lot of time together, but she always listened and tried to help. It had been good to have a girlfriend again even if it hadn't lasted long. I was over the moon that Luc remained on Earth with me, and we could finally be together, but it had been nice having a girlfriend to talk to again when she'd been around.

Luc's family, affected by the divine, hadn't worried much about him, strangely. His dad was away on work a lot, his siblings were older and didn't live in the house anymore, and his mom had been burned out from his presence. He planned to graduate a semester early and move out on his own "for college" soon, so his family could get back to normal.

He and I started to sneak into the devastated theater to get away, like we used to when we skipped classes before, except now we had to climb through crumbled wreckage and dodge construction workers. While it was dangerous, I never felt threatened with him there. We had a lot of work to do; finding out where the initial demon outbreak had begun, investigating the bombsite, and seeking out any remaining fallen angels. We'd determined from our regular talks with the angels

~ ☾ ~

upstairs that no one else had seen or remembered slaying Evil Barbie Hillary in the battle either.

"She has the Spirit Sword," Luc explained. "She's fallen, angry, and has a holy weapon. It's something we need to be on alert for. Not to mention the fact that the bomb was set so close to the theater, which is where the majority of the angels met regularly."

"The demon knew you."

He nodded. "Which means we know him."

While we could communicate with the angels and archangels above, Luc needed to figure out a way to communicate with any guardians still posted on Earth. He struggled with this for some time, until I showed him how to create Facebook groups. Once we had a group, with help from the archangels and a few Heaven to Earth missions to locate all of the remaining guardians, the Earthly communication was taken care of.

I beamed at him after setting it up.

"You are amazing." He kissed me.

"At least I have the communication thing under control for Heaven and everybody, don't I?"

He spun me around in my office chair at my computer, his smile fading.

Luc took my hand and kissed it, lingering on the ring he'd given me.

I smiled back at him.

"I didn't get to tell you this at the time, but you know it's a Claddagh ring. It's an Irish symbol of friendship, which is how we started, love, which is where we are now, and loyalty. If you look closely," he said bending down next to me and pointing at the ring, sending butterflies all over my insides, "you can see the hands with the heart between them make up one part of a cross, and the crown down is the other."

"It protected me from the demons."

"I'm not sure if you've thought much about this since

Speak of the Devil

everything happened, but you have had more than one guardian assigned to you."

I nodded.

"Mike and me," he said.

"Mo?" I asked. "He saved me."

"Possibly Mo. Possibly Vi, and if you think about it, several guardians have intervened or tried to help you for one reason or another."

"Belle, the junior guardians — they tried to keep me from the seniors when they thought you were falling." I thought about it "Why do you think that is? I mean, why me?"

He took a deep breath. "I don't know exactly, nor do Rafe or Kristabel. But we do know it's extremely rare. You're one of the very few humans to ever be allowed to know the ins and outs of our celestial circle. Plus, you're currently our Chief Communications Officer." He grinned briefly, and then his roguish smirk faded.

"I'm a regular Lt. Uhura."

"You're our only line of communication to Heaven."

"What does it all mean?"

"Again, we don't know for sure, but we do know it's important. You're special." He held my hand and stroked it softly with his thumb. "There is talk though." He paused.

"Yes?"

"You may be the key."

"To?"

He pursed his lips and took a while before speaking. "To finding God again."

"What?" I frowned. That was crazy.

He shrugged. "You may be our only hope, our Princess Leia so to speak." He grinned.

"Then you're screwed," I teased.

"Everything happens for a reason," he said cryptically.

~ ☾ ~

"I'm just glad you're here and all of my angels have done such a good job protecting me."

He remained serious at this, a cloud coming over him for several minutes, before his deep green eyes met mine, and his famous smirk reappeared. I put my arms around him and kissed him without guilt or worry or sadness. The waves of warmth and the familiar feel washed over me.

He pulled back from our kiss and grinned. I must have been glowing. "Mmmmm," he murmured.

"Your kisses are heavenly," I told him.

He scoffed, but it was true. I knew because I'd been there.

~ ☾ ~

Epilogue

    She trembled as they left the theater hand in hand, and bile rose in her throat. They were always there. In the theater. Her theater. She could finally relax as they walked away with their sickening young love stench wafting away with them. While she hadn't heard if they'd found anything out, she thought she should report what she knew. She made her way to the green room back stage and sat at the make up table. She took a deep breath upon seeing the antique mirror placed above the table, as she always did. Its ornate, gold leaf carvings wrapping themselves around its surface. She reached out to it, tracing a finger along the lines of its frame before one more deep breath set her back to her task. Staring at her reflection in the mirror made her grin. She took her thick, horn-rimmed glasses off and repined the butterfly barrettes to tame her frazzled hair before taking some reddish-brown lipstick out of the make up table and putting some on.
    She loathed those kids, avoiding them as much as possible, but it was so difficult when they always hung out in the theater, sometimes all day. She should report them for skipping classes, but didn't want to draw unnecessary attention.
    She pulled the tray of make up out of the center drawer, revealing a circled star decorated in various runes and drawn in something that matched her lipstick. She took a deep breath and placed her hand in the middle of the circle, making it illuminate.
    "Lucifer," she whispered, and a shadowy face

~ ☾ ~

appeared in the mirror. "Too many survived and they're starting to snoop around—"

"I know. Unlike God, I'm not silent or absent. Ever." His deep voice reverberated through her, and Ms. McNair shook as a nervous anxiety seized her.

Author Bio:

Shawna grew up in and around farms in the heart of Missouri but attended University of Kansas. She now lives in Nova Scotia with her husband, two sons, two rescue dogs and one overgrown puppy from hell. She's a non-conformist who follows her heart.

She has her BA in creative writing from the University of Kansas where one of her plays was chosen to be produced locally, and two of her short stories were published. She earned her MA in English from Central Missouri State University where she wrote a novel as her thesis.

She's taught English at the university and secondary levels for nearly twenty years and can't quite fathom how all her students have grown up, yet she's managed to stay the same. She's a huge geek and fan of Xena, Buffy and all kick ass women, and loves to write stories that have strong female characters.

CPSIA information can be obtained at www.ICGtesting.com
Printed in the USA
LVOW130634050313

322647LV00001B/18/P